The Last of
the High Kings

Also by Ferdia Mac Anna

Novels
The Ship Inspector
Cartoon City

Memoirs
The Rocky Years: Story of a (Almost) Legend
Last of the Bald Heads: A Memoir

Editor
An Anthology of Irish Comic Writing

About the Author

Born in Dublin, Ferdia Mac Anna has worked as a television producer and director, journalist, magazine editor and scriptwriter. For some years he toured Ireland as lead singer and songwriter with Rocky De Valera and the Gravediggers, and later The Rhythm Kings. He was producer and script editor on the acclaimed award-winning BBC/RTÉ children's drama series, 'Custer's Last Stand-Up' which won a BAFTA for best drama series.

He has written numerous plays and screenplays and has published two other novels, *The Ship Inspector* and *Cartoon City*. His memoir, *The Rocky Years*, was published in 2006 by Hodder Headline and is in development for a TV drama series. He has also taught at a number of colleges and universities, including DCU, NUI Maynooth and IADT, where he currently lectures on Screenwriting and TV and Radio Broadcasting. He works as a freelance TV producer, director and writer on Dramas, Sitcoms, Documentaries, and Soaps.

THE LAST OF THE HIGH KINGS
This edition published 2011 by
New Island
2 Brookside
Dundrum Road
Dublin 14

First published by Michael Joseph 1991

www..newisland.ie

ISBN 978-1- 8484-0106-8

British Library Cataloguing Data. A CIP catalogue record for this book
is available from the British Library

Book cover and typesetting by Mariel Deegan.
Printed by Drukarnia Skleniarz

New Island received financial assistance from
The Arts Council (An Comhairle Ealaíon), Dublin, Ireland

10 9 8 7 6 5 4 3 2

Ferdia Mac Anna

The Last of the High Kings

NEW ISLAND

To Kate

and with thanks to Dom

I am just a cowboy, lonesome on the trail.
The starry night, a campfire light...
The coyote calls and the howling winds wail.
So I ride out to the old sundown...

- from 'The Cowboy Song' by Phil Lynott

1

FRANKIE

Frankie woke up drunk.

But he sobered up fast when he found that he couldn't move. He was paralysed, he thought. He'd had a stroke. It was all over. There was something heavy on top of him, holding him down. He lay in bed, imprisoned by his own bedclothes, wondering what was going on.

A stiff piece of paper was stuck to his face. He twisted until he could reach it with his fingers. It came away with a loud 'striiiick'. As he moved, a heavy rustle of stuff slid to the floor, freeing him. Frankie sat up and looked at the paper in his hand. It was oddly familiar. One side had a design he recognised. The other was white and somewhat sticky. Piles of similar bits were scattered all over his bed and on the floor.

Then he looked at the walls of his room. They were stripped and gouged and ripped free of wallpaper. Only a few isolated streaks remained. Even the poster of bare-chested Jim Morrison of The Doors, the one that usually glared down at him every morning from the centre of the wall opposite, had vanished.

Frankie's younger brother Ray, sitting up in the other bed, watched to see what his brother was going to do. He could see that Frankie was confused.

'Last night, you found a bit sticking out,' Ray explained, 'so you pulled that off. Then another bit stuck out, so you ripped that off too. Then you went all round the room tearing off all the bits that were sticking out...'

Frankie held the piece of paper in his hand and examined it. Then he looked at the walls again.

'Fuck's sake.' Frankie said.

'I saved Jim Morrison. He's under your bed.'

Frankie didn't know what to say. He couldn't remember tearing the wallpaper. He couldn't remember getting into bed either. But he did remember the bottle of tequila, and sitting in the front seat upstairs on the last double-decker hill bus home with Hopper Delaney. The bus had been stuffed with teenagers coming back from the tennis club dance. Frankie's next-door neighbour had been sitting two seats behind. Now it was coming back to him and playing in his head like a bad pop song. He closed his eyes.

'Anyway,' Ray chirped, 'Ma came in this morning, saw what you'd done and dumped the whole lot on your bed.'

Ray thought for a while.

'I think Ma's annoyed,' he said with jolly deliberation. Ray reckoned he was pretty smart for a twelve year old.

But Frankie was back on the last bus, watching himself in a horror movie. He and Hopper had on their best blue denim jackets and were smoking white-tipped cigars. They blew gusts of black smoke from their mouths when they laughed. From time to time, they passed the bottle of tequila to each other, taking huge lipsmacking slugs as though it were lemonade. Drinking tequila on the last bus home was great gas, they thought.

Upstairs, most of the laughing, chattering teenagers were drunk, or at least merry. Some were singing 'Tie a Yellow Ribbon Round the Old Oak Tree'. There were a few sombre drunken adults scattered about, but they were only upstairs because they'd been too slow to grab a seat downstairs where the sober people sat.

Everyone was surprised when Frankie was sick. He threw up onto the floor just as the bus turned the corner by the Abbey Bar and began its ascent of the hill. Some people even stopped singing.

Frankie was a bit surprised himself, but there was nothing he could do about it. As the bus tilted, people sitting behind had to raise their feet as Frankie's mess slid by.

'Aw here, what's this?' the man sitting behind Frankie said.

'Mother of Jaysus,' said the teenage boy behind him.

Hopper tried to help, but Frankie was bent double convulsing up his guts, so Hopper gently removed the bottle from Frankie's grasp and raised his own feet.

When Frankie had finished puking, he put his cigar out. The last thing he remembered was the bus conductor coming upstairs, stepping in something slippery, then taking a long, disgusted look at his shoes before scooting back down without bothering to collect fares. Today, the whole road would know about it.

Frankie pushed back the bedclothes and untangled his bare legs. Slowly, he lowered his feet onto the floor. He looked across at Ray. Ray looked at the wall.

'Do you remember what you did with Parnell?' Ray asked.

'Parnell...?' Frankie said.

Frankie was trying to figure out what he had done to the dog when the door of the room burst open. Ma stood in the doorway with her eyes tightly blazing and a cigarette in her mouth. Her anger flew across the room and slapped Frankie across the face. He grabbed the bedclothes around him.

'Noelie's gone, get up you and get him,' she said to Frankie.

Then she spun on her heel, as if offended by being in the same room as her wayward son, and walked on down the corridor. She left the door hanging open, as always.

Frankie got up and fumbled in the debris for his clothes. He found his blue jeans under a pile of wallpaper and his denim shirt wedged between the windowsill and the bed. It took him ages to pick the little bits of wallpaper out of them and get dressed. Then he couldn't find his socks.

Ray picked one of his little red notebooks off his bedside chair and opened it. In his spare time, Ray wrote novels. He kept them in a stack by the side of his bed and re-read them when he ran out of comics. He and Frankie had an unspoken arrangement: Ray did not watch Frankie dressing, and Frankie did not interfere with Ray's novels.

Frankie wasn't drunk or hung over now. He was just stunned. The sunlight through the window made him feel worse. In its beam, millions of dust paratroopers were dropping to the floor. The room looked as though it had thrown itself at him. He certainly didn't feel like asking Ray any more questions about last night.

Frankie grabbed his denim jacket, left the bedroom, and walked down the corridor to the kitchen where he found Ma by the sink staring out at the sunshine. The kitchen was even more untidy than usual: chairs were skewed at awkward angles along the sides of the kitchen table like bumper cars at a funfair, while all the cups and saucers that were usually stacked in piles on the dresser were, for some reason, spread out on the floor along with several tins, a bag of groceries and a floppy mop. As he stood there, shafts of sunlight splayed around Ma's head, flaring her long red hair ghostly white at the edges as they flickered across the strewn china like the torches of cinema ushers. A row of capless black Guinness bottles stood to attention on the window-ledge like toy soldiers who had lost their heads. At Ma's elbow, a transistor babbled.

'Bomb in Belfast,' she said, without looking. 'Two Brits dead, thank God.'

'Where's Noelie?' Frankie asked.

'Aah, he was playing on the back wall. He's probably in Macken's field now, or up at the Summit.'

Ma wouldn't look at him and obviously wasn't going to give him breakfast, so Frankie left to look for his young brother.

Outside, the sunshine made his head ache. His long black hair felt clammy against his neck and cheeks. It was impossible to take in the beauty of the day, or enjoy the spectacle of the sloping green fields twinkling in the heat haze all the way down to the shiny blue sea and the island beyond. The heat made him aware that he was too tall, too skinny and too pimply-faced to ever amount to anything. He did not feel like a healthy seventeen year old who lived on top of Hill Road with his Ma and Da and two sisters and two brothers and dog, Parnell. Nor did it seem as though he had his whole life ahead of him. Instead, he felt as though a badger had died in his stomach.

He picked his way down the steps by the front window, along the little footpath separating the porch from the front garden, and onto the driveway. He walked down the tilting tarmac past the shattered wooden post that had been glorious white-painted gates until last Friday afternoon when Da had come home in a bad mood and driven the car straight through them. Frankie and Ray had been kicking a ball around in the front garden when they heard a crunch and watched a shower of splinters rising over the hedge like confetti. Afterwards, Da had shrugged his massive shoulders and casually explained that he'd grown sick and tired of always having to get out of the car at the bottom of the drive just to open the bloody gates. Now the problem was solved, he had explained. At the time, Frankie and Ray had thought it perfectly reasonable—until Da had ordered them to clean up the mess.

Right now, Frankie wanted to run away, leave his parents, brothers, sisters, Dublin, Ireland and Parnell for ever. Maybe he'd try California. Over there, he'd heard, the girls were tall and had tanned legs.

Frankie had no money, no summer job, no prospects of travel. He didn't even have a girlfriend. Da had promised to 'talk' to him about going to university in September, but Frankie was sure he had failed his Leaving Cert exams, which was a drag because university seemed like such perfect freedom. Getting into university would mean that he would be finally clear of sarcastic teachers whose job it was to make young people feel stupid, and clear of brutal Christian Brothers who would rather whack you on the head with a wooden duster than teach you anything. He would be away from his parents too, which would be a relief the way they were carrying on these days.

As he thought about it, he realised that he had been looking forward to a lot of things about college, from sharing a flat in Rathmines and studying English, or maybe History, and reading loads of books, to being in a place where his height wouldn't matter because everyone with half a mind would be able to see that brains were what really counted. He would meet girls there—smart, beautiful girls with white teeth and blonde hair, who would talk to him about Hemingway and The Stranglers and fall about laughing at all his jokes.

European History had put a stop to that. The paper had consisted of all the questions that the history teacher had assured the class were too obvious to come up and therefore not worth studying. After an hour of struggle, Frankie had come to a question that asked: 'How Absolute was Louis XIV?' 'Very Absolute', Frankie had written, and walked out.

The English exam had been worse. He had misjudged the time and left an hour early. Realising his mistake, he had tried to go back in, but the Head Brotherdone—a bespectacled ape with a crewcut whose favourite method of torture was to lift boys off their feet by their ears—had just sneered and told him he was 'well and truly up the Swanee now'.

The memory made him uneasy. So did his recollections of last night. Now he could recall sitting on the front porch in the early hours with Parnell cradled lovingly on his lap, and singing 'If You Were the Only Dog in the World, and I Was the Only Boy...' He had given the dog a saucer of tequila. After that, Parnell had sung too. Lights had gone on all over the hill. Neighbours had yelled. Other dogs had joined in. Midway through the third verse, Da had come out in his pyjamas and taken the bottle away. 'Go to bed this instant,' he had boomed, 'or else sleep in the feckin' coalshed!'

If he didn't get into university, he would head for California, he decided. Whatever happened, this would definitely be his last summer at home, he promised himself.

On the green opposite the Summit pub, Vinnie Cassidy, Jack the Rack and some of the other Big Guys were playing football. All around the makeshift pitch, families were picnicking on blankets. As he drew closer, Frankie could see clumps of people sitting at the tables outside the pub.

At a table nearest the green, Noelie was trying to wrestle a pint of Guinness out of the grasp of an old man.

'Aaaaah, aah,' Noelie said.

'Get off, will ye?' the old man snarled. 'It's my shaggin' pint!'

By the time Frankie reached Noelie, half the old man's pint had been slopped onto the ground. Noelie was glad to see Frankie though.

'Hello, Frak,' he said, grinning. 'Kick footba'?'

Frankie promised that they'd kick football as soon as they got home. Then he took Noelie by the hand and led him away. Noelie waved goodbye to the old man, who clutched what was left of his pint and pretended not to notice.

2
CLARA

In the beginning, there was a three-prong plug.

He found it under a chair when he was crawling. It was big and white and had sharp edges and three golden prongs which tasted funny. It was the most fantastic thing he'd ever seen. He decided to show it to Ma. But Ma was walking across the room, not looking at him. She was about to leave. So he threw it to her as hard as he could. The plug hit the side of Ma's head with a dull 'twock'. She gave a little 'oh' and crumped up on the floor like an old cloak, just as Da came in the door. He helped Ma to her feet. Red-faced and snarling, Da pointed at him. 'Someday, I'm going to sling that feckin' wah out the window!' he roared.

'Feckin' wah' was a bit extreme. Usually he was just a wah. Whenever he was particularly bold or cried loudly or acted the maggot, Da called him a 'bloody wah' or 'that little so-and-so.' However, when he was good he was 'Francis.' If he was looking especially cute, they called him 'Frankie.' It was a bit confusing. As soon as he learned to talk, he was going to give out shite about it.

He learned to say 'Ma-ma' and 'Da-da' and 'ball' and 'apple.' Ma tried to teach him to say 'Massachusetts.' 'Mama-chew-chuf,' he said. Ma laughed and told him what a good boy he was. He wondered what a Mama-chew-chuf was. Eventually, he decided it was another name for Ma. Da must be Dada-chew-chuf, he figured.

At the harbour there was always a biting breeze, and lapping water, and the crackly cawing of gulls overhead. Even when the sun was shining, it was cold. The men on the fishing boats wore woollen hats with coloured bobbles on top and bellowed with raucous, hollow voices to their mates on the pier. He wanted a hat with a bobble on it, so he pointed at one. 'Yes, boats,' Ma said, 'very good.' On walks, people often bent down to look at him and tickle his chin and talk baby-talk. 'Say Massachusetts,' Ma would say and at first he did and everyone always laughed and told Ma what a grand boy he was. After a while, though, he got fed up saying Massachusetts. He tried other words instead. Words like 'Feckit,' just the way Da said it. Soon people gave up asking him to say things.

One summer's day, Ma took him for a stroll along the pier. He remembered leaning out to examine the different types of seaweed that clung to the wooden walls. Next thing he knew, he was under the water, his hands trying to reach up to the inky figures that swirled above on the pier. It was like a dream. He was almost sorry when a fisherman jumped in and saved him. Back on shore, Ma slapped him hard on the bottom. 'I can't leave you alone for a moment,' she said. He bawled. As he was whisked away, he caught a glimpse of the fisherman's bobble hat twirling away towards the centre of the harbour.

At home, Ma told him he was a special boy, descended from the ancient Celtic warriors and High Kings. She said there was powerful blood in his veins because he was the firstborn son. Someday he'd be a great man, she promised; he'd be a professor of history, then President of Ireland. That kind of talk made him feel great. Every time Ma leaned over him he felt warm and secure and lightheaded. It was like being bathed in his own personal spotlight.

He was just getting used to things when Ma went away for a while and brought home a new wah. She told him it was his baby sister. Da put it in his old crib. Ma had gone to a lot of trouble to give him someone to play with, Da explained. He tried playing with it, but the tiny baldy thing just lay there and made gurgling noises. He poked it with his plastic Viking sword. It burst into loud wails and got him banned from the room. He went right off the cute wee bundle after that. It really annoyed him when visitors kept going on about its beautiful blonde curls and gorgeous blue eyes. As far as he was concerned, there was only room for one wah in this house.

The first act was to pour a bottle of milk into the baby's crib. It was kind of interesting to watch its expression change. Ma caught him and hauled him into the study to Da. Da slapped him and took away his Viking sword. 'You'll get it back as soon as you learn to behave,' he was told. His big move came one morning when Ma took them to the Summit shops for groceries. He was put in charge of the pram while Ma went inside. He considered for a while, then released the wheelbrake and gave the pram a push. It trundled off down the pavement and bobbled onto the road, picking up speed as it headed downhill. Ma came rushing out just in time to see the pram merging into the traffic. Someone caught the pram a couple of hundred yards down the hill but not before Ma had fainted onto the eggs.

At home afterwards, with Da shouting at him and Ma whingeing and clutching the baby, he let on to be ashamed. Inside, though, he glowed like a hot-water bottle. It was nice to be in the centre of the spotlight again.

When his sister Maggie was older, he persuaded her to eat a couple of Ma's cigarettes. She was sick for a week, but she didn't die. He was very disappointed: Ma had always assured him that cigarettes were deadly for kids.

He hit his sister and his sister hit back. Sometimes they threw things and once she brained him with a biscuit tin. Ma was always declaring that one or other of them had disgraced the family. When they ran out of things to fight over, they fought over who had disgraced the family most. 'You don't deserve a mother like me,' Ma said, 'you're going to give me cancer, I know it.'

Finally, to keep things quiet, Da told them about their big sister Clara who lived in the attic. She had been banished there before they were born for being very very bold. The same thing would happen to them if they didn't wise up. After that, they mentioned Clara only in whispers. It was like having a stranger in the house. Lying in bed late at night when the house was quiet and there was no traffic going up or down the hill, they were positive they heard scuffling noises overhead. Once, playing in the driveway, Frankie was sure he caught a glimpse of a face in the attic window. In dreams, he imagined a small figure in a cloudy smock with a pale smudgy face and blonde curls.

Eventually, his sister dared him to go into the attic and see for himself. 'Why should I?' he asked.

'You're chicken,' she barged.

'Am not.'

'Are so.'

'Amn't.'

'Are...'

'OK, OK,' he said finally, 'now you'll see.' Tremblingly, he climbed the ladder to the attic, feeling like a condemned convict. He lifted the creaky trapdoor, then jerked the flashlight beam across the dusty floorboards. It took him a few moments to realise that there was no trace of Clara. Not so much as a blanket. As his confidence returned, he was disappointed to see that there wasn't even a rat. Nevertheless, his sister refused to climb the ladder to see for herself.

'I believe you,' she said, 'just come down and close the trapdoor, will you?'

At night, though, he still heard scuffling noises overhead. He didn't mention it to anyone. Whenever Da and Ma gave out to him about something and sent him to his room, he lay on his bed and imagined sneaking up to the attic to talk to Clara about things. It always made him feel better. It became his big, glorious secret.

One night, he was dreaming about playing hopscotch in the attic with Clara when Da suddenly shook him awake and took him by the hand to the front porch where flickers of light ran up and down the front walls and lit up the garden like heat haze in summertime. The house across the road was burning down. Sparkling red fire-engines winked at him through the gaps in the front hedge. 'Have a good look,' Da said, 'you might never see anything like this again.' Da sounded almost pleased. So he stood on the cold porch in his bare feet with Da's huge hands on his bony shoulders and looked. Ma brought his sister out and the family stood watching the flames. After a short while, he felt guilty. He looked up at Da with a fearful expression on his face. 'What's up?' Da asked. 'I didn't mean to do it,' Frankie said, 'I swear I didn't.' Da laughed so hard the walls across the road caved in and millions of sparks shot up into the night like rockets.

At breakfast next morning, Da ushered everyone into the study. When they were all seated, he creaked forward on the black leather armchair and plucked a shiny disc from the record rack at his feet. He placed it carefully on the red, wooden gramophone. 'Listen to this,' he said. They hushed and listened to *Madame Butterfly*. Da conducted the singing and explained the story during the orchestral parts. They kept quiet because they knew that music was a lot more important than Mass or new clothes or dinner or even the news on TV. Da closed his eyes and sang along in a soft, high voice. Music made Da happier than anything. At the end, everyone wanted to hear it again. So Da played it again. They all sang and hummed along and waved their hands in the air just like Da.

Other nights, Da sang along to Harry Belafonte or Joan Baez. He sang 'Day-O' and 'Brown Skinned Girl' and 'Copper Kettle' and 'The Night They Drove Old Dixie Down'. He liked to bounce the kids on his knee to 'I Want to Hold Your Hand' by The Beatles. Maggie was his blonde yokibus, Frankie was his little anarchist. When Maggie got measles, Da stayed up with her at nights and sang 'Scarlet Ribbons' to her until she got better.

The arrival of a brother, Ray, came as a big shock to Frankie. Someone was getting in the way of his personal spotlight again. 'Now you'll really have someone to play with,' Da said. 'Don't want anyone,' he said sulkily, 'can play all right by myself.' As soon as Ray was able to walk, he had him up the back kicking a football. It made a change from fighting with Maggie all the time. Sometimes, Da came lumbering up the back and went into goal and the boys took shots at him. Dad was so big, nothing got past. Ray was able to kick the ball like a proper footballer by the time Noelie arrived. 'Wahs, wahs everywhere,' Da said, 'we're building a football team.' Ma said Noelie was the best looking of the lot; it was obvious that he was destined to be a great soldier or statesman.

The night Noelie got sick, everyone ran around the house in their dressing-gowns. A doctor came but could do nothing. Ma's face was like chalk. She sobbed into a hanky that Da gave her. Da and Ma carried Noelie to the car to take him to hospital. The kids stood on the porch, and watched the small red tail-lights fading down the black drive. Mrs Donovan from down the road looked after them for the night and made them their breakfast next morning. Da came home at teatime. His face had turned the same colour as Ma's. Noelie was in a coma, Da explained; it meant he couldn't wake up. Ma was taking it very hard. He wanted everyone to be extra good until Noelie got better.

Noelie didn't wake up for most of the school year. When he did, he had permanent brain damage.

By the time Noelie came home, everyone knew that their little brother would never be normal; Noelie's body would grow up, but his mind could not. 'Every family has a cross to bear,' Ma said, 'Noelie is ours.'

A year later, Dawn was born. Nobody was expecting her, not even Ma. Everyone said that Dawn was the cutest baby girl they had ever seen. 'It's God 's way of making up,' Da said, 'everything will be all right now.'

Dawn was a year old when Granny and Auntie Lucy and Uncle Louis arrived one night to take her away with them. Granny was white-haired and craggy-faced and bigger than most men, bigger even than Da. Everyone was a bit afraid of her. Behind her back, Da called her the Rumpus Gran. The Rumpus Gran held her head as straight as a queen but spoke from the corner of her a mouth like a TV gangster. 'It's for the best,' she told Ma, 'you obviously can't cope. I passed Francis in the hall and his clothes are filthy, an absolute disgrace. And Maggie needs a new dress for school and Ray's hair is walking off him with the dirt.' 'Yes,' Auntie Lucy said, 'and it's not as if you're losing Dawn—you can visit any time you want and at Christmas and Eastertime too.' Ma couldn't speak. Da stared at his in-laws to see if they were for real. 'It's the only way,' the Rumpus Gran said, 'after what you let happen to poor little Noelie.'

Ma broke down as Da reared up from the old leather chair and ordered them to get out of his house. 'Indeed, I will most certainly not,' the Rumpus Gran said and folded her arms, 'how dare you.' Da picked her up in his massive arms, chair and all. 'Get your hands off me, you blackguard,' she shrieked. 'Help, police, police, I'm being assaulted!' Da lugged her to the front door, somehow managed to yank it open and tossed her out. 'Steady on,' said Uncle Louis, who was always saying things like that. Da threw him out on his ear. 'At least let us have Dawn,' Auntie Lucy wailed as Da dragged her through the hall, 'it's for her own good, the poor little creature.' Da pushed her out too and slammed the front door on the lot of them.

'You'll rot in hell for this!' the Rumpus Gran shouted through the letterbox. 'Oh feck off out of here,' Da said, and dropped their handbags out of the study window. 'Stupid people,' Da said, 'don't mind them, they can't touch us.' He patted his kids on the head one by one to stop them shaking. Then he went back into the study to comfort Ma.

After that, Da often went away to act in plays in Paris and London and New York. Ma explained that Da had to go abroad to get enough money for Noelie's special school and to pay for their food and the house and the car. She said they should be proud of their father, that the name of Proinsias Griffin was known and respected throughout the acting world.

From London, Da sent them packets of Opal Fruits. They got bars of rich dark chocolate from Berlin and, from New York, Hershey bars in crackly wrappers. By the time the packages arrived, the chocolate had usually melted into a thick black goo inside the wrapping but nobody minded—it was exciting to get a package through the post from somewhere far away. But Frankie missed the sing-songs. Hearing any kind of music when Da was away just made him feel empty inside. It also made the sweets taste funny.

He made friends with Huey who lived at the bottom of the road. In the mornings, they walked to school together. Huey was a pudgy, slow-talking boy with a square, friendly face and a crew cut. He was always in good humour. They swapped toys: Huey borrowed his six-shooters and he got Huey's Action Man. 'These are lendies, not keepies,' Huey warned. Once, they sat down at the bus-stop outside the town library and figured out their lives. 'When I get big, I'm going to be a prospector,' Huey decided. 'I'll look for gold in Wyoming.' 'Well, I'm going to be a professor of history,' Frankie said. 'After all,' he explained, 'a descendant of the High Kings of Tara has a duty to become a professor of something.' Later, he confided that history was boring and that he'd much prefer to be a prospector too. They made a pact to go to Wyoming together someday.

In school, they sat in different classrooms. But they saw each other at breaks and always walked up the hill together when school was over. Sometimes he went to Huey's for his tea. At gym one morning, during a game of leap-frog, Huey collapsed. The games teacher put him on a table and tried to revive him, but Huey was dead. 'His heart just stopped,' the teacher said. The Head Brother came to reassure them. 'It's a tragedy,' he said gravely, 'no one could have foreseen it.' 'Please sir,' a boy said, 'I think I know who killed him.' The boy was taken aside for a talk. Everyone was sent back into the classroom while they took Huey away.

After school, Frankie walked up the hill alone. He felt numb and lonely. As he passed Huey's house, he wondered if he should knock and give back the Action Man. At home, Ma sat him down at the table and put a plate of fish fingers and beans in front of him. 'Huey died today,' he said. But Ma was busy; the phone was jangling in the hallway, Maggie and her friend Jo were having a fight under the table and now the pan had caught fire. 'Eat your tea or you'll get spots,' Ma said.

In school, nobody bothered him much because he was tall and gangly and sulky-looking. Everyone was too busy beating the crap out of the smaller boys. Tall guys were too much hassle. The Christian Brothers were wary of him too. He was the son of a famous actor. They didn't want any trouble. During classes, he looked out of the window. Or stared at the pretty squiggles on the blackboard until his mind whisked him away. Now and again, he was caught daydreaming. The Head Brother called him a 'long, lanky, lazy lubradán'. The maths teacher referred to him as a 'waster' and a 'gombeen'. That was OK, he figured: he would rather be a lubradán or a gombeen any day than a Christian Brother. He carried on making movies in his head.

One lunchtime, during a game of Fisherman's Net, he got into a fight with a squat, red-headed boy who butted him in the jaw. A front tooth popped out. Everyone stopped to examine it. 'Sorry about that,' said the boy, 'I meant to loaf you on the nose.' He shrugged it off. 'It's all right, I'll grow another one.' The red-headed boy's name was Daniel Delaney. He was small and dumpy and wore thick-rimmed glasses that never fell off. Everyone called him Hopper because he couldn't sit still, not even during Religious Knowledge class which usually put everyone else to sleep. He and Frankie became pals.

A week later, they were expelled for painting a Hitler moustache and fringe plus swastikas on the statue of the Virgin Mary which saluted visitors, arm stiffly outstretched in blessing, at the school entrance. They were readmitted only after both sets of parents had agreed to double their voluntary contributions to the school's building fund. Back in school, their first assignment was to scrub every inch of the Virgin Mary until it sparkled. 'This is all your fault,' Hopper said. 'I told you not to leave your fucking initials on it.'

3
HILLYBILLYS

One afternoon, Ma sent him to the Summit shops to buy her twenty Carrolls and two bottles of Guinness. On the way home, two boys pushed him to the ground and demanded money. He refused, and the boys started kicking him. Suddenly a wiry, sharp-nosed boy with a fierce expression on his face and long, straw-coloured hair waded in and knocked the boys' heads together The boys ran off. 'Howarya,' said the newcomer, 'I'm Nelson Fitzgerald and I live just up the road. Gimme sixpence or I'll break your face.'

Within a few days, they got tired of fighting each other. They became friends instead. Nelson was handy to have around. He wasn't afraid of anyone. Even some of the big guys were scared of him. Nelson knew all the secret back paths and boreens. He could run fast and jump high walls and kick over his own head and ride a bike down the hill to the town without using his hands—or the brakes. He was a great goalie too. He puffed out his cheeks and made spectacular dives to save the simplest shots.

They formed a gang. They called themselves 'The Hill Gang', but everyone else called them 'The Hillybillys'. They played football matches against 'The Townies' and hung around the Summit acting tough. That summer, they started gorse fires and then claimed the ten-bob rewards for reporting them. One day, the wind changed suddenly and they had to run for their lives. After that, they gave up starting gorse fires.

They developed a special high-pitched yodel. 'Owoo-ow-oo-ah,' it went. Whenever they wished to summon one another, they simply went out to their back gardens and yodelled. The yodels were heard all over the hill. On a clear day, the sound reached the harbour. At teatime, a sudden burst of yodelling often made neighbours spill pots of tea and once a man who lived down the road accidentally stabbed himself in the side with a carving knife. Finally the police told them to cut it out. It was either that or become the first kids in history to be jailed for yodelling, the sergeant said.

That halloween, they climbed onto the roof of a retired British major's house and dropped hangers down his chimney. The fireworks exploded in his fireplace just like grenades. The major thought they sounded real, too. He came out after them with a shotgun.

When they got older, they hung around the cliff beach. Sometimes they built rafts. Mostly, though, they lay on the scorching rocks with all their clothes on and drove themselves mad watching Romy Casey and Jayne Wayne and Jennie Brady and the rest of the hill girls swimming and sunbathing and lolling around the strand in skimpy bikinis.

Nelson was going to be a fisherman someday, he boasted. He would work on the boats every summer and save up his money until he had enough to buy his own boat. Then he wouldn't have to take orders from anyone. 'I'd be me own skipper,' he said dreamily, 'people would have to do as I say or get shagged overboard.' Nelson thought Frankie's Ma was real good-looking. 'Are you sure she's not your big sister?' he kept asking. 'I'd really fancy her if she wasn't your Ma.'

They played cowboys and Indians on the old tramtracks which wound their way up the hill from the town and ended opposite the Summit pub. The tracks were hidden from the road by masses of bushes and rows of wild ferns. There were hideaways and ditches and holes and fields on either side. Adults rarely came there, so Frankie and Nelson, Hopper Delaney and Cyril McLean the lighthouse-keeper's son, and the rest of the hill kids could make as much noise and play there as long as they liked. Years before, the Big Guys had dug up all the brass and metal tramlines and fittings and sold them. Nelson said that Jack the Rack had made so much money that he had been drunk for a year, and Bobby Gallo had even bought a motorbike.

Halfway along the tracks, there was a deep groove in the ground that looked like a crater and was ideal for Custer's Last Stand. When they got bored with cowboys, they switched to Nazis versus US Marines. One of their favourite games was called Stalingrad. Nelson was the Russian Army and the others played the surrounded Germans. The game ended when Nelson had killed everyone.

Nelson was the undisputed leader of the Hill Gang. He was tall and fierce and would bust anyone who gave him any trouble. Usually they played whatever he felt like playing. No matter how action-packed the game, nobody ever shot Nelson.

Sometimes, Jack the Rack and Vinnie Cassidy and the other Big Guys invaded the tracks and chased the Hill Gang home. Vinnie Cassidy loved to take Frankie's guns, dip them in cow dung, and toss them far into the fields. 'Someday, I'm going to fucking kill you!' Frankie shouted at him one day. Vinnie hit him a box on the ear. 'Oh yeah, you and whose army?' he jeered. Once, Frankie picked up a stick and whacked Vinnie in the gob with it while Vinnie was laughing. Vinnie threw Frankie over a fence. When the Big Guys had gone, they found one of Vinnie's teeth on the ground. Nelson said it was the only time anyone had ever persuaded Vinnie to part with something belonging to him. After that, even Vinnie's friends called him Gaptooth.

One day, as Nelson was leading a detachment of US cavalry along the tracks hunting for signs of the Apaches, Jack the Rack appeared. Jack the Rack wore a cowboy hat and carried a real-looking Winchester. Jack was four years older than them, had a beer belly and a red nose, and was always acting the hardman outside the Summit pub. He liked to boast that he carried a hatchet under his jacket. Nobody objected when he announced that he was Kit Carson, official US cavalry scout. He knew the Apaches' movements, he said; if they followed him, they could sneak up on their camp and wipe them out. It seemed weird to have a fifteen-year-old leading a bunch of eleven-year-olds but everyone went along with it. It was better than getting a hatchet in the mush, Nelson whispered.

Jack was deadly serious. He made them crawl along a muddy ditch until they came upon the Apache camp which was hidden behind a clump of green and yellowing bushes. He raised his Winchester and they rode in whooping and shooting. It was the greatest battle they'd ever fought: they shot down thousands of ferocious Apaches; they got knocked down and picked themselves up a hundred times; there were growling gunshots and whanging ricochets and frantic cries of 'look out' and 'help' and 'aaaagh' and high-pitched Indian war-whoops of 'woo-woo-woo' and 'ah-ooh-ah-ooh-ah' and brutal windmilling close-quarters fistfights. Cowboys and cavalry got wounded in the arm but kept firing. There was intense competition among the Apaches to see who could come up with the most spectacular death fall.

Towards the end, little Cyril McLean climbed on top of a high rock, held his hands to his chest, and contorted his face in agony. 'They got me, men, look after Martha and the kids,' he yelled before toppling. By Dusk, even Nelson had been killed at least a dozen times.

It was Frankie who noticed that the new scout was missing. They formed a posse to look for him. Eventually they came upon Kit Carson lying face down in a hollow with raspberry juice smeared across his lips and a hand outstretched into a puddle of water. The Winchester was stuck barrel first into the earth beside him like a leaning flagpole. Everyone thought it was the most touching thing they'd ever seen. That's the way to die, Frankie thought, not during a stupid game of leap-frog in a school yard.

Next day, Jack was back with his mates hanging around outside the Summit pub. As they passed on their way to the tracks, Jack ignored them. Later, he and Vinnie invaded the tracks and chased them off. Jack never showed up to play again. 'Those eejits never change,' Nelson said. 'When I grow up, I'm going to burst every one of them.'

'Not if I burst them first,' Frankie said.

Every time Da came back from America he brought Frankie a record. One summer Frankie got The Doors' first album. Next, it was John and Yoko's 'Sometime in New York City'. Another time, Da gave him 'The Allman Bros Live at the Fillmore East'. Frankie wrote down all his possessions in a big ledger. Soon he had over twenty LPs and a small portable record player. Later he added lists of books that he'd read: Ernest Hemingway, John Creasey, Richard Brautigan, Zane Grey, Herman Hesse. He read James Bond books for the sexy bits, but he didn't bother listing those. He grew his hair. He wore floppy sandals, flared jeans and cheesecloth shirts. He developed spots. He grew his hair longer to hide the spots. Sometimes he forgot to wash. At school, the French teacher called him a 'sale poisson'. He was too intimidated to ask what it meant. Later someone explained that it was the French for dirty fish. He said he didn't care, he'd rather be a dirty fish than a French teacher any day. After that, whenever a teacher made sarcastic remarks to him, he imagined himself as long-haired Duane Allman, lead guitarist with the Allman Brothers, playing brilliant guitar solos on stage at the Fillmore East. He missed a lot of classes whilst playing music in his head.

At home Ma gave out to him about everything. She said his hair was a disgrace. She didn't like his clothes or his habits or his friends—except for Nelson who was a nobleman from a noble family and would never dream of giving his mother cheek. She forbade him to go to the tennis club dance. He snuck out and got drunk and went anyway. When he got home, there was a row and Ma threw a cup at him. 'That's all I ever get from you—trouble from the moment you were born,' she wailed.

In bed afterwards, he felt guilty and cold and worthless. To escape the bad feelings, he thought about Romy Casey from six doors down. He drifted off into a dream in which she climbed in through his open window and danced ring-a-rosy around his bed in her short summer dress, bare arms glinting in the moonlight. He dreamed that she slipped into bed beside him and put her soft warm hand on his thing. 'Hello, what's this?' she giggled. When he awoke, his stomach and balls were wet and sticky. He could feel stuff oozing from the top of his penis. God, it's bleeding, he panicked, I'm going to die. In a little while, he calmed down enough to begin stroking himself. He was stiff as a pole. He thought about Romy Casey and her dark eyes and thin lips and long, long legs. Sensations began to build in his belly and tingles ran down the insides of his thighs. It was exciting, pulling at himself in the pitch darkness, feeling power swelling in him. The rhythm made soft clapping noises, like ponies trotting on a beach. He hoped it wouldn't wake Ray in the next bed.

It was ages before his little volcano blew. He was amazed by the way the stuff went cool on his skin almost immediately. He used a sock to clean it up.

Afterwards he felt doomed. The Christian Brother who hammered biology into their skulls in school had been very clear about this sort of thing; if it happens by itself then that's natural, but if you touch it then that's a mortal sin.

He had touched it, he had touched it, he had most grievously touched it.

Cautiously, he licked a wet fingertip. It had a bitter, tangy flavour, like sour cream. His terror frittered away. Now he knew what a mortal sin tasted like.

At the weekends, they listened to Elvis and The Beatles and had arguments about who was best. Elvis was always best because Nelson threatened to mangle anyone who said he wasn't. On Saturday nights, they went to the tennis club hops. 'What'dye get? What'dye get?' they asked each other afterwards. 'Just a wear,' Frankie lied. 'No use, I got a feel,' Nelson boasted. 'Well, I got me hole,' little Cyril McLean bragged. 'How'd ye manage that?' Nelson said, 'you must have stuck it in a Coke bottle.' Once Hopper got slapped across the face for accidentally touching a girl's breast during a slow dance, He never bothered asking anyone again after that. Instead, he sat in the corner and made remarks about the girls the others asked.

One night, Nelson danced with pretty little red-haired Patty Gargan from the town. She jumped up on him and wrapped her legs around his waist and he swung her about to the music. They danced every dance like that. After the hop, Patty made Nelson give her a jockey-back all the way home. 'Go on, giddy-up, Bigfella!' she yelled. The others followed to see what was going to happen. At her door, Patty got down and gave him a long kiss. On the way back up the hill, Nelson's fierce expression was gone and his eyes were lit up. 'One day soon, I'm going to marry that girl,' he said, 'just you wait and see.'

'But you're only fifteen,' Frankie said. 'I know what I'm doing,' Nelson barked. That was the last time Nelson ever discussed his private life.

For Frankie's sixteenth birthday, Da gave him a pair of goldfish in a large bowl. 'Keep them in the kitchen,' Da said, 'they'll brighten up the place.' 'Er, thanks,' Frankie said. 'You have to change the water every day,' Da instructed, 'and make sure you don't give them too much food or they'll eat themselves to death.' Then Da went off to London for three months to play Polonius in *Hamlet*. The day after Da had left,

Ma tried to get Frankie to join the army. 'But I don't want to be a soldier,' he protested. 'I still have a year of school left.' 'The army will school you,' Ma said, and phoned for a taxi to take them to the recruiting centre. He locked himself in the bathroom, squeezed out through the narrow window, and raced up the back fields to Nelson's house. When he came home that evening, Ma gave him a look. 'God help Ireland if she ever has to rely on the likes of you,' she told him.

At Christmas, Da came home and Ma cooked the biggest turkey in Dublin. 'We'll be eating it for a month,' she proclaimed proudly. Frankie was given the task of bringing the steaming bird into the dining-room on a large silver platter. But Maggie got in his way and he slipped. The turkey skidded across the kitchen floor and thudded against the back door. Ma called him a fool and whacked him on the backside with the carving fork. 'Right, that's it,' he said. He opened the back door and kicked the turkey out into the snow just as Da came charging into the kitchen with his teeth bared and his arms out like a grizzly bear. Frankie ran for it. The goldfish bowl missed his head by inches and exploded on the wall of the shed.

An hour later, when everyone except Ma had calmed down, Frankie and Da picked up the broken glass and searched for the goldfish. Both were still alive. One had landed in the bin and the other lay flopping in a pool of melting snow. After putting the goldfish into cups of water, they went back into the yard and stood looking down at the Christmas turkey. It was embedded in a mound of slushy snow.

'You can't really blame it,' Da said, 'it was only making a last desperate bid for freedom.' That night it was so cold that Frankie couldn't sleep. In the small hours, he heard the door of his room creak open. He pretended to be asleep. Ma took his heavy greatcoat off the back of the door, then padded across to his bed. She spread the greatcoat on top of his blankets and tucked it into the sides. The weight pressing down on him made him feel warm and secure and snug. Ma padded out and closed the door and he went to sleep.

He dreamed that he was up in the attic with Clara. They played pattacake, pattacake baker's man and one-potato, two-potato. Clara showed him her dollies, then poured him an imaginary cup of tea from her toy teapot. When it was time for him to go, she smiled a sparkly smile at him and told him in a sweet voice that he could visit her again if he liked. He promised that he would, just as soon as he was able. Then he opened the attic hatch, climbed down the ladder, and went back to his room.

4
DALEKS

Frankie was kicking a football around in the front garden with Ray and Nelson Fitzgerald when a Dalek roared up over the hedge. Its long bulbous scanning-eye and its metal death-ray were focused on them. The ball flew past Frankie's head and whacked into a bush.

'Mother of Moses,' Nelson said.

They watched as the Dalek sailed up the driveway on the roof of Da's Austin Cambridge. Kites of black smoke from the exhaust fluttered behind. It looked like a spaceship landing.

When the car stopped in front of the garage, the Dalek wobbled like an old drunk and, for a moment, it leaned backwards as though about to topple and roll off.

Then it settled, standing tall and cone-shaped and secure, except for the rounded head which swivelled slowly around until the scanner was pointing back the way it had come. Six-year-old Dawn stood with her mouth open on the front porch, dolly dangling from her tiny hand.

'Gorney,' she said.

Da got out of the car, glanced up at the Dalek on the roof, smiled and stretched. He turned to face the kids and shrugged his massive shoulders.

'Now, waggles,' he said, and walked up the path to the porch steps with his head down and his arms pumping like pistons.

He passed Ray who ran up to the car and stood gazing up at the Dalek. 'Is it ours?' he asked.

'Yes, but go easy, it might have to go back to the theatre some day.'

Ray began to untie the knots in the ropes which held the Dalek in place just as Mary Figgis from next door peeped over the wall. Mary Figgis said nothing, simply stared through her thick round glasses as she always did whenever there was the slightest thing to look at. Ray stopped untying the Dalek and gave her the finger. Mary Figgis went away.

Frankie and Nelson left the garden and ambled over to the car. They walked slowly. Frankie feigned interest in the grass, the pathway, the bright blue cloudless sky, the neat green bushes along the side of the drive. He didn't wish to appear over-excited just because there was a Dalek in the middle of the driveway on top of his Da's car.

'It's just like on "Doctor Who",' Dawn said, and raised her dolly to give it a clear view.

There was a splatter of dishes from inside the house, followed by flurrying footsteps. Ma loomed out of the front doorway. She leaned forward and peered white-faced and wide-eyed over Dawn's fair head. Her gaze took in the boys, her husband, and finally the tall rounded alien on the roof of the family car. At first Ma's face was stern and uncomprehending, as if she thought someone were playing a trick on her. Then she saw the smile on her husband's face as he came lumbering up the porch steps, so she smiled too.

'Oh, Proinsias, that's wonderful,' she said, then dipped her head to the level of Dawn's ear. 'What is it?'

'It's a Dar-lek, Mammy. It annihilates people.'

'Oh.'

Ray tried to get the others to help lift the Dalek off the roof. Frankie was reluctant to exert himself because he didn't want to look stupid or undignified. Nelson said that it wasn't his Dalek and he didn't want to be held responsible if they dropped it and it broke. So Nelson stood back and watched as Ray struggled with the Dalek alone. He folded his arms and gave slit-eyed mocking glances down his long thin freckled nose. After a while, Nelson got on Frankie's nerves and brother decided to help brother.

Eventually, the Dalek was hauled off the roof and deposited on the sloping tarmac where it swayed and creaked. The new arrival was six feet high and made of bright balsa wood. It was wide at the base, sloping up to a smooth round robot top. The inside was hollow and had a narrow slit in the head for a person to see out. All the futuristic coloured baubles on the outside were made of plastic except for the death-ray—a long tube of metal with holes in it that reminded Frankie of Ma's cheese-grater.

When they took their hands away, the Dalek trundled off by itself. They had to grab hold to keep it from rolling off down the driveway. Nelson still refused to have anything to do with it.

'It's fucken possessed,' he said.

But when they lifted it and examined the base, they found dozens of small steel rollers. Even Nelson was impressed. They put it down, and poked and prodded and pawed the outside to see what it felt like. Ray kicked it on the side a couple of times.

'Testing for strength,' he explained.

Nelson was interested now, despite himself. He assisted with the pushing and the pulling. The Dalek was even more awkward than it looked. It was a lot heavier, too.

By the time they had manoeuvred it off the driveway, along the narrow cobbled path, through the gap in the hedge and into the front garden, all three were exhausted.

As soon as they got their breath back, an argument started about who should get first go. Ray felt it should be him because he had done most of the work. Frankie said he should go first because he was older. Nelson declared that he was toughest so he was going first and he would burst anyone who tried to stop him. Frankie said that it was a family Dalek so family should go first—Nelson could get his own Dalek.

'Oh yeah?' Nelson said.

'Yeah' Frankie said.

They stared at each other.

Ray tried to sneak in while they weren't looking but Frankie caught him by the ear before he could get underneath the raised base.

'Ow, gettoff,' Ray squealed. 'I was just looking.'

Dawn came down from the porch and wanted to play too. Then Noelie came walking along the wall. The moment he saw the Dalek he wanted it. He made soft anxious crying sounds as he climbed down into the garden. Maggie appeared on the front doorstep to see what all the fuss was about. She drifted out to the edge of the porch with her hippy pals, Mo and Jo. They stood in their flared jeans and kaftans, giggling and sneering at the weird object in the garden that the others were fighting over. Frankie thought they looked as though a flock of sheep had exploded on them.

Maggie thought everything her older brother did was stupid. His clothes were stupid, his friends were stupid, and the music he liked was stupid, especially those crappy All-man Brothers records he kept playing on his tacky portable record player. But this Dalek in the garden was the stupid-est thing she'd ever seen in her life, she said. Mo and Jo agreed.

'Just look at it will you?' Maggie said. 'It's stew-pit.'

After staring down at everyone for a few moments, Mag-gie 'humphed' loudly for the boys to hear and flounced back into the house in a twirl of golden curls and swishing kaftan, followed by Mo and Jo.

Frankie shrugged scornfully. 'You'd think she'd know by now that kaftans are out,' he said. 'This is 1977 for fuck's sake.'

'Yeah, fuck's sake' Ray agreed and quickly sidestepped to dodge a clout.

Everyone took it in turns to go inside the Dalek. Nelson went first—because Frankie didn't feel like having his nose broken. Then Frankie himself went, and finally Ray. They ignored Dawn and Noelie.

The others grew bored quickly and gave it up, but Ray clanked and cranked around the bumpy garden, jangling the death-ray and scanner and making alien noises.

'Annihilate the human beings. Anni-hil-ate, anni-hil-ate!' he shouted before the Dalek plunged into the hedge and had to be rescued.

Ray's enthusiasm gave Frankie an idea. 'Hey, this is great. We can hire it out to all the kids on the hill and make a packet. We'll form a Dalek Rental Agency.'

'I don't know about that,' Nelson said. 'You wouldn't get me inside that thing again if you paid me.'

In a little while, Nelson said he had better things to do with his life than stand around watching a rickety old wooden dummy space-machine, and went home.

At teatime, Ma had to call them three times before they gave up playing with the Dalek and came in. Dawn wanted to know if she could go back out and bring the Dalek in for its tea too, but Ma told her to forget it.

'Daleks probably don't like sausages anyway,' Dawn said.

There was smoke in the kitchen as usual, so Ma opened the back door to let in the air. Parnell came in too, pink tongue lolling. The dog saw Frankie, padded over to him and leaped up to lick his face and be petted, but Frankie pushed it off. Frankie had gone off Parnell since the other morning when he had found the dog lapping water out of the toilet bowl.

Ma held a fig roll in the air over Parnell, then dropped it. The dog caught the biscuit in its mouth and chewed it noisily.

One side of the table was wedged into the wall. Ray and Frankie sat at one end, Maggie and Dawn the other, and Noelie sat in the middle. Ma took the warm plates of rashers and sausages and fried eggs from the stove and clattered them out on the table. She delivered Da's tea to him in the study—as she always did. Then she got her own plate and sat on the high stool by the sink, her back to the table where Dawn and Ray were making faces at each other and Noelie was attempting to cram the butter dish into his mouth.

Frankie took the butter dish out of Noelie's hands and put it out of reach. He barely noticed his food. He was day-dreaming about the money he'd make renting the Dalek out for rich kids' parties. He would hire it out to the local seafood festivals too. There was no end to the wealth-making schemes. The Dalek would make him a fortune. Now he wouldn't have to look for a summer job.

Ma stared out of the window and smoked a cigarette. Occasionally, she poked a fork into a sausage and sighed. Ceili music gushed from the radio. Nobody looked at anyone else as they ate, except Noelie who looked at everyone.

'Hello, Frak,' Noelie said and Frankie said, 'Hello, Noelie, good fella,' and carefully removed the bits of fried egg Noelie had thrown onto his plate.

All around the kitchen, jars and cans and bottles and packets were crammed onto sideboards and ledges and into cupboards, jammed against stacks of dishes and rows of cups and saucers and mugs. There were onions on the sink rest, cans of Heinz beans on top of the radio, and a bag of potatoes under the kitchen table. Now and again, a foot sent a spud scuttling across the blue linoed floor. Nobody picked it up.

On the grey walls hung photos and posters and charts and newspaper cuttings. Some had peeled outwards and looked ready to fall. Over the door was a selection of stills from the various shows Da had acted in over the years. Many were of Ma and Da in younger days. A few showed them in full stage costume and make-up. A pile of crumpled clothing lay in the corner. It was waiting for Frankie to take it up the back and hang on the line. The pile had been waiting for two days.

As he chewed a rasher, Frankie decided to escape once tea was over. He would wander out into the back yard as if going for a stretch and then scarper up the back garden, over the wall and across the fields to Nelson's house; there he'd watch TV or play records until it got dark. He was too old now to be hanging washing.

Suddenly, Noelie stood up and started jumping up and down to the céilí music. At first everyone tried to get him to cut it out but he kept jumping and chanting 'yi, yi, yi', a big smile on his face.

Ray got up and said, 'Well, what the hell.' He jumped up and down and chanted 'yi, yi, yi' as well. Dawn did the same. Noelie laughed. Dawn laughed. Everyone laughed, even Ma. Parnell barked.

Maggie got up and joined in. Then Ma leaped off her stool, got in the middle of the carry-on and held Noelie's hand as she jumped up and down with him. Ma's face lit up. She looked like a wild young girl.

'Come on, you,' she said to Frankie. 'Don't be an old spoilsport.'

Grumpily, Frankie got up and started jumping too.

After tea, Ma nailed Frankie just as he was sliding out the door. It took half an hour to hang all the washing on the back line. When he'd finished, Ma called him a 'good boy'. That really pissed Frankie off; he was seventeen years old going on eighteen, but Ma treated him like a child. Being called a 'good boy' just made him feel really worthless. It meant that all the girls on the hill were too stylish and sexy and rich for the likes of him who never seemed to have much money and didn't drive a car—not even Da's car—and didn't even own a motorbike—not even a Honda 50—but always took buses and sometimes missed the last one from the city and had to walk ten miles home.

He didn't even own a wallet or a guitar or a decent stereo system. It made him think that he was never going to grow up. He was relying on university to save him. Once he got into college he wouldn't have Ma nagging him or Maggie sneering or Ray making smart remarks. But then he remembered the

Leaving Cert exams and that made him depressed again. As far as he was concerned, his life was over if he failed his exams. If that happened, he figured he might as well go away—to California, for ever.

He went back into the front garden to see what the others were up to. It was past seven, but there was still plenty of daylight. Ray was inside the Dalek, chasing Dawn and Parnell around the garden. Noelie was kneeling on the bank of the driveway, tossing rocks out into the passing traffic.

Frankie joined in the game. They took turns inside the Dalek. But Frankie's heart wasn't in it. Inside, the air was hot and stale and sweaty. Manoeuvring was awkward—whenever he turned too fast, he scraped his head against a jutting bolt or angle. It was no fun.

To liven things up, Frankie suggested they bring the Dalek onto the driveway and see if they could control its movements on the slope. It would be great gas, he said; it would come in handy when they were renting it out. Ray would be like a test pilot, daring to boldly go where no other twelve-year-old had ever gone before. Frankie promised his brother shares in the Dalek Rental Agency once it got going. Ray hesitated at first, but Frankie soon talked him into it.

'I am not chicken,' Ray said.

'OK, let's see you then.'

Getting the Dalek out of the garden with Ray inside and without Nelson to help was difficult. Pushing it along the cobbled path was murder. Ray roared that he wanted out but Frankie told him to hang on, they were nearly there. At the junction of path and driveway, the Dalek stalled. Ray refused to go any farther.

'It's too heavy!' he shouted.

'Scaredy-cat,' Frankie said and gave the Dalek a gentle shove.

The tiny rollers jingled into a momentum of their own. The Dalek rolled forward.

'Hey,' Ray said. 'Now quit messin', OK?'

The Dalek tilted abruptly onto the tarmac and then scuttled off down the driveway. It rapidly picked up speed. As it began to spin, it made a sound like a thunderstorm. The scanner flapped like a cow's tail. Frankie ran after it. Dawn ran after Frankie. Parnell ran after everyone.

Ray yelled like a banshee. The Dalek crashed into the white gatepost at the bottom of the driveway. It spun and toppled over. Ray was tossed out across the tarmac like a wet shirt. He hit the far bank with a plop.

Frankie pulled up and watched in horror as the Dalek rumbled into the road, leaving a trail of broken bits behind. There was a sudden screech of brakes as a car swerved to avoid it.

Noelie jumped up and down on the bank above. He got so excited he threw a rock into the Figgises' garden.

Ray hauled himself up and glared at his big brother. He was winded and mud-splattered and red-faced and sore all over. He didn't want to be a test pilot any more.

The shattered hulk of the Dalek rattled against the far kerb. Pieces were scattered across the road and up as far as the white posts of the driveway. The death-ray lay mangled on the white line in the centre of the road. Cars beeped as they drove by.

This is not the way things should have worked out, Frankie thought.

At that moment, dark-haired Romy Casey from six doors down, the most beautiful girl on the hill, walked by. She looked down at the smashed-up Dalek, then turned to give Frankie a playful smile before walking on. Frankie had never felt so mortified.

Dawn turned and ran back up towards the house. 'Mammy, Mammy,' she screeched, 'Francis is after killing the Dar-lek.'

That night he dreamt that he flew down to the harbour to see how the boats were doing. He drifted overhead for a while, watching the swaying masts and listening to the clinking of the tiny bells and the swish of the easy surges of water against the pier walls. When the mood took him, he dipped down to skim the mouth of the harbour, to feel the spray pitter-patter across his face and taste salt on his lips. Then he headed out across the winking waves to the dark mass of the island beyond. It was glorious to feel the buffeting wind on his bare skin, filling his mouth and nostrils and making his lungs inflate like balloons as the island loomed out of the water like a great whale.

At regular intervals, the white beam from the lighthouse flared across his path, blasting through the blackness to reveal the white-caps beneath and bony rocks jutting up. From out there, the entire head was lit up like a fairground. He could follow the orange blips of the streetlights along the seafront road into the town and up along the winding way to the top of the hill to the white-walled bungalow where he lived. It felt good to be out in the blackness, flying.

In a short while, he knew he would soar back across the waves and above the gaping jaws of the harbour. He would fly over the gently rocking boats and up past the shops and pubs and tiny pale houses. He would tip with his hand the top of the spire of the smoky black church at the end of Main Street before zooming up glistening, dark, wet-nosed Hill Road with his arms out, fingers touching the billowing trees that leaned towards him. He would hug the bends and twists in the road and keep his eyes squinted against the wind until he reached home. The last bit was always easy. He would swoop up the tilting driveway, clear the red-tiled roof of the house and drop like a leaf to land on his bedroom windowsill to feel the morning dew soaking into the soles of his bare feet. Nothing to it. When morning came, he would open his eyes to see the wounds in the wallpaper where the poster of bare-chested Jim Morrison used to stare down at him. He would stretch out a hand to the chair beside the bed and feel around for his clothes.

In the meantime, he was lord of the world.

5
COWBOYS

Ma gave out to Frankie for not getting off his arse and finding himself a summer job. After that, Da called him a 'long-haired chancer'. Frankie got fed up being harassed. He decided to run away. After tea, he slipped out of the back door and scooted across the back fields to Nelson Fitzgerald's. He and Nelson stayed up until two playing Elvis records, then he bedded down on an old mattress in Nelson's room.

'Nobody at home understands me,' Frankie told Nelson. 'I hate them all and I'm never going back. Tomorrow morning, I'm heading for California.'

'Don't forget to write,' Nelson said and went to sleep.

Frankie went home at noon next day. Nobody mentioned his absence. Everyone was too busy searching for Dawn's cat, Buster, who had been missing for over two days.

'Maybe Parnell 'et him,' Ray said.

'Don't be thick,' Maggie said. 'Parnell's scared of cats.'

'Yeah, what else could you expect from a dog that only eats fig rolls?'

Ma sent Frankie up to the Summit for a baby Powers and ten Carrolls. When he returned she told him to help look for Buster.

'Ah, Ma!' Frankie protested. 'That Buster is a psycho. Dawn can go and find it herself.'

'Ooooh, of course, that's typical. You always try to get out of anything you're asked to do, don't you? Well, it just won't work this time, mister. Just find that child's cat—*now, if you please*.'

Dawn was convinced that Buster had been kidnapped by Mary Figgis from next door. She wanted Frankie and Ray to go over there right away and get Buster back.

'He's a good cat, he'd never run away without telling me.'

Ray was on for it. He drew a map of the Figgis house and put large Xs on the spots where he figured their defences were weak. Then he stood up and hooked his thumbs in his belt like John Wayne.

'If he doesn't show up in half an hour, we're goin' in.'

Frankie ambled around the back garden and kicked rocks. He spent a lot of time gazing over the back wall. He hoped that Buster had been squished by a truck. That would save a lot of hassle.

No trace of Buster was found in the garden or alongside the house. Ma sent Frankie, Maggie and Dawn to rummage in their own rooms while Ray was ordered to search the living-room and study.

Frankie found a pile of red notebooks under Ray's bed— Ray's treasured novels. Ray usually wrote at least one a week. When he was feeling down, though, the output doubled. Ray boasted that a true writer always produced his best work when he was depressed. Ma loved to tell people that he was the best twelve-year-old novelist in the world. Only last week

Da had praised Ray's latest novel, a western entitled *Satan's Saint*. Da had pronounced it a 'first-class read'.

Ray had gone around with a smug face on him for ages. Finally, Frankie had had to take him up the back garden and push his nose into the sandpit a couple of dozen times to get him back to normal.

Frankie sifted through the red notebooks until he found *Satan's Saint*. He stuck it into his belt, covered it with his shirt, and put the remainder of the novels back where he'd found them. After dinner, he would see what all the fuss was about.

Just before dinnertime, Maggie heard meowing coming from the airing cupboard in the kitchen. Inside, she found Buster curled up on a pillow with four blindeyed kittens crying all over it. Everyone gathered to examine the scene. Noelie tried to snatch a kitten but Ma took him by the hand and led him outside. Then she ordered Ray to take him for a long walk.

'Ask anyone you meet if they want a kitten,' she shouted after them.

Dawn studied her cat. Her pale six-year-old brows tightened. 'Buster's a girl,' she announced finally.

'Congratulations, kid,' Maggie said. 'The world is full of surprises.'

SATAN'S SAINT

Chapter 1

The dust was raising on the plain. The dust was from two horses that galloped across the sand at breakneck speed. One was ahead of the other but the other was closing in fast. Two puffs of smoke came from their hoofs. Suddenly a sandstorm came out of the desert. The first man's horse tripped and he sprawled on the sand. The other man rode up to him and stopped. The mounted man drew his gun and pointed it at the man on the ground. The muzzle spat flame and death and the man's life sped from him. He rolled over and lay still. The mounted man rode off and the sandstorm buried the dead body.

Chapter 2

The sandstorm blew into a small town called Vulture Gulch. Tumbleweed rolled past the locked doors and shut windows. Sand rattled against the windows as if it was trying to get in. In a certain house down the street lived a sheriff by the name of Wyatt, Bart Wyatt. His deputy, Paul Hindman, lived with him.

Hindman moved to the coffee pot and poured a cup of coffee and gave it to Wyatt. 'Thanks pard,' Wyatt said in a deep prairie voice and drank the coffee down. Hindman started a conversation by stating the fact that they had not caught the desperado who had been operating for weeks in the desert around Vulture Gulch. The sheriff said, 'Sure, how can we go after him with this sandstorm on? We'll raise a posse after the storm and get on his trail.'

'I don't see how we can when its gonna be all covered with sand,' said Hindman, scratching one of his granite jaws.

'Well, let's hope our deputy Hops Malone can give us some information on him.'

Little did they know that Hops Malone was lying under a pile of sand because he knew too much and had to be dealt with.

Chapter 3

The killer of Hops Malone rode into town just as the storm died down. The killer was called Luke Odell and everyone in the West had heard about his vicious exploits. Luke Odell parked his horse at the hitching-rail and moseyed on into the Hangman's Neck saloon with a mighty thirst on his lips. 'Whiskey and leave the bottle,' he told the barman with great cruelty the moment he reached the counter. The cowpokes at the bar were scared stiff with fright.

Odell was a tall man, not necessarily lean. He had a crooked nose and the skin was etched tight around his mouth which made him look even more evil than he really was. He had two dark eyes which, if you looked at them closely, you would swear never blinked. Very few men ever looked at them closely and lived to tell the tale. He swallowed down the whiskey with long gurgling gulps, his Adam's apple bounding up and down. After he had that done, he sat down at a table and smilingly slammed his massive hand down on a small fly that was walking about on the tablecloth.

As he sat there drinking loudly, the town clerk, a mister Myron Barrington, entered the bar and ordered a glass of milk in a refined tone. No sooner had the barman handed over the glass of milk than a violent guffaw shattered the otherwise stillness of the saloon. It was such a fierce guffaw that nobody thought about going for their guns. Barrington turned around and adjusted his spectacles to see who was laughing at him.

'Am I to believe, sir, that you were laughing at me?' said the tender clerk who had been coming to the saloon to drink milk for many years, and who most people regarded as one of the finest clerks to ever draw breath.

Luke Odell stood up, the empty whiskey bottle dangling monstrously from his venomous hand. 'I sure am,' said Odell with another earth-shattering guffaw.

Odell strode over with a menacing swagger that made everyone in the bar fear for the little clerk's safety. He took Barrington's glass of milk and poured it ruthlessly over the tender clerk's shoes, which were only shoes and not boots like all cowboys wear. Barrington jumped back as the cold milk bit deeply into his feet.

'You are nothing but a saddle tramp and a whiskey bum!' Barrington shouted with as much dignity as he could muster.

'Oh-oh, now you gone and done it little man,' Odell said grinningly. 'Let's see you back up your big words with your tiny fists.' So saying, he stamped his boot down viciously on Barrington's toe. The thunderous stomp and the yell of complete shock were blended together as one. Barrington almost wept with the sheer agony of the excruciation.

'All right, you're asking for it,' Myron Barrington said and swung a punch that was meant for Odell's massive protruding nose. But Odell sidestepped and Barrington's skinny fist flew past. Odell ducked under and drove a hard left to Barrington's delicate chin. The tender clerk shot through the air and landed about five feet away. All the cowpokes at the bar said 'ooooh.'

As the little clerk was bravely trying to rise, Odell drew his gun and put six bullets into him. Barrington sighed once and lay back down. Odell blew smoke from the barrel of his gun and went over to the still body of the defenceless little town clerk he had just gunned down in cold blood. He glanced violently at the body. 'This here squirt is dead,' he yawned in a matter-of-fact way. The cowpokes at the bar removed their stetsons.

A little later, the bat-wing doors of the saloon swung open and a dark figure with fancy guns on his hips appeared in the shadow thrown by the chandelier. 'Mister,' the figure said in a deep prairie voice, 'you plumb picked the wrong day to cause trouble in my town.'

The shadowy figure moved out of the murk into the light. Everyone went 'oooh' again for the figure was none other than Bart Wyatt himself, sheriff of this small but peaceable town of Vulture Gulch, Wyoming. Wyatt was well known for being the most violent lawman in these parts. They said his father had been a gunslinger from Dodge, and some swore that his mother was the secret daughter of the great Red Indian chief Cochise. Bart Wyatt had been a gunslinger himself, but had stopped it because of the senseless killing. Now he believed in truth, honour, integrity, justice and happiness for all decent cowboys.

Wyatt had the look of a born fighter about him. He had big fists and small beady eyes. His nose was large but winsome. When he moved it seemed slow but his muscles were as taut as whipcord under the rawhide waistcoat. He wore two pearl-handled pistols on a pearl-studded gunbelt which was filled with rows of silver bullets. Two jagged knives hung from his gunbelt and there was a derringer in his waistcoat pocket which nobody knew about. He walked with a wry purpose that showed he knew where he was heading and what he was going to do when he got there.

'Ah don't cotton to wicked acts especially killing for no reason so Ah'm a gonna take you in,' said sheriff Bart Wyatt. He moved past the prone, motionless, lifeless body of the dead little town clerk mister Myron Barrington who had only been looking for a glass of milk and didn't deserve to be lying there with six bullets in him.

'You ain't taking me no place, marshall,' Luke Odell roared. Bart Wyatt walked to where Luke Odell stood chuckling and drove his huge clenched fist into Odell's giggling yellow teeth. Odell, taken completely by surprise, staggered back. 'Doggoned varmint,' he said as he spat teeth and blood onto the floor.

Odell swung a big bunch of knuckles that was called a fist into Bart Wyatt's handsome features. Wyatt spun and crashed into the bar and broke a rake of glasses. Quick as a flash, Odell scooped up a fallen chair and smashed it over the sheriff's arched back. Wyatt got winded and fell to his knees before toppling onto his face and lying there grunting softly to himself with blood streaming from his nose. All the cowpokes could see that Wyatt's back was a mass of bruises under his shirt. Odell moved in and reached for his six-gun. It looked like tombstones for sheriff Bart Wyatt.

Suddenly Bart Wyatt jumped to his feet and kicked the six-gun out of Odell's hand. Then he slammed an enormous fist into Odell's vast nose. Odell went reeling over two tables and a chair and bounced off the bar counter before glancing off the piano and landing on top of another table with a gigantic tinkle. When he landed, Odell didn't get up any more.

Now everyone could see that sheriff Bart Wyatt was one tough hombre. The sheriff smiled a wry smile as he took the jail keys out of his pocket. 'OK,' he said to the cowpokes at the bar, 'you've had your fun. Now go on home.' The cowpokes shuffled off one by one with shamed red faces, clutching their stetsons. Wyatt picked Odell off the floor and put the handcuffs on him and locked the handcuffs tight with the jail keys. 'Ah'm a taking you in for the murder of the town clerk, as good a man as ever drew breath,' he said in his deep prairie accent.

All the fire had gone out of Luke Odell's black eyes. He didn't remember committing the wicked act. He also didn't recall gunning down Hops Malone in the desert. In his mind, he had no idea how the little town clerk got to be lying on the floor of the saloon with six bullets that he didn't deserve in him. It was a very puzzled face that Luke Odell wore as he was pushed out of the Hangman's Neck saloon towards the jailhouse by sheriff Bart Wyatt.

Note: All characters are just fiction and not based on anyone I know personally including my older brother. I

hope you enjoyed this sheriff Bart Wyatt story as much
as I enjoyed writing it. I hope you didn't mind the blood
as I had to put it in because of realism. I have to end my
author's note now. Goodbye until next time.

Yours truly, Raymond Griffin, author of The Guns of
Sheriff Burns, Spy's Playground and Five Mad Mexican
Gunslingers.

Frankie closed the red notebook and threw it on his
brother's bed. Now he no longer cared if Ray found out that
he had been reading the novels. He didn't think much of
Ray's stuff anyhow. He couldn't see what Da had been raving
about. Sure, the murderer didn't even get killed at the end.
The sheriff led him away in handcuffs. What a load of crap.
Anyone who knew the slightest thing about the real Wild
West knew that handcuffs were just not on. Any bad guy
worth his salt would have been carried out of that saloon feet
first. That proved that Ray wasn't a serious writer. If he had
had any sense, he would have had the whole lot of them die
in a big saloon shoot-out. That would have been more believ-
able, he reckoned. Reading the novel had made him mad.
First chance he got, he decided, he was going to hit Ray a box
in the mouth. That would teach him who was the real tough
guy around here.

In the morning, Noelie scalded a kitten with the hot water
that Ma had boiled for the breakfast tea. Ma told Frankie to
take the poor little creature up the back and drown it. Frankie
started to protest but Ma just shrugged. 'It has to be done
and you're the eldest so you have to do it.'

The kitten looked to be in a bad way. Its fur was scorched
off in places and its eyes were shut tight. From time to time,
it emitted a thin meow. Frankie wrapped it up in an old tea
towel and carried it out. Everyone followed Frankie up the

back garden to watch him drown the kitten. Frankie held the bundle out in front of him and pretended not to notice the others. Behind him, Ray brought a tub of water and a battered plastic bucket and spade. Maggie flounced in front in her straggly kaftan.

'You haven't the guts,' she jeered.

Frankie ignored her and walked on. He felt the kitten trembling inside the towel. Dawn fluttered alongside, craning to get a look.

Frankie had never drowned anything before. He tried to look tough but it was difficult to act like a hard man when you were about to kill a defenceless kitten. Ma had told him to do it, he argued to himself, so it must be OK. He sneaked a look inside the bundle. The kitten's neck was red and raw-looking and there was stuff oozing from its eyes. Yes, it was in bits. Ending its misery was the only merciful thing to do.

They reached the back wall and stopped and stood around, looking at one another.

'I suppose we better say a few words,' Ray said piously.

'Don't be thick,' Maggie said. 'He hasn't killed it yet.'

'We could let it go,' Dawn suggested.

'No,' Frankie stated firmly, 'it's too far gone. We have to put it out of its agony.'

'Yeah,' Ray said, 'it's only humane.'

'It is not humane,' Dawn cried. 'It's a kitten.'

Ray raised his eyebrows and looked at the sky. 'Maybe we should drown you instead,' he said to Dawn, who shrugged.

Dawn thought for a moment. 'We could get it a doctor.'

'Cats don't have doctors, silly,' Maggie snorted, 'they have vets.'

'Well, a vet then.'

'Oh, God.'

Frankie knelt and laid the bundle on the grass. Ray put the tub at Frankie's feet. Slowly and carefully, Frankie unwrapped the towel. The kitten spilled out onto the grass. Its fur was matted and there were yellow blotches around its eyes. Other than that it didn't look too bad. Once the sunshine hit its face though, it meowed weakly.

'Let's get it a brain surgeon,' Maggie said sarcastically.

'Yeah,' Dawn said, then frowned. 'What's a brain sturgeon?'

'Shut up, or I'll put you up in the attic with Clara.'

Dawn turned pale and shut up.

The kitten meowed again. Frankie lifted it and held it over the tub at arm's length. Suddenly he wasn't sure what to do. If he dropped it in, it might just float on top and make him look stupid. He'd have to hold it under to make sure. But then the kitten might scratch his hand. There had to be another way.

'Go on then, get it over with,' Ray said.

'Yah, he can't,' Maggie said.

'Shut your face, barge.'

'Frankie-wankey,' Maggie sneered.

'Bargey-wargey.'

'Wankey.'

Frankie had an idea. 'Gimme that,' he said, and grabbed the plastic bucket from Ray's hand.

Frankie dumped the kitten into the bucket. In one movement, he turned the bucket over and plunged it into the tub. Water splashed on his knees but he didn't care. He pressed the bucket to the bottom with both hands until his arms ached. After the water settled he noticed that he had forgotten to roll up his sleeves. Beside him, Maggie and Ray were strangling themselves with giggles.

'Serves you right, picking on a poor defenceless little kitten,' Maggie said.

When Frankie pulled the bucket out the kitten was still dry as a bone. Astonished, they watched as it attempted to crawl up the side.

'I think you missed,' Ray said mockingly.

Quickly, Frankie spun the bucket over and splashed it in again.

This time, he held it under for nearly two minutes, But when he removed it, the kitten was only slightly wet. He held the bucket over the water and shook hard but the kitten dug its claws into the sides and refused to fall out.

'Weee-ow,' it wailed.

Maggie laughed. Ray smiled as though he knew something the others didn't. Frankie just felt weak. Dawn was delighted.

'It's a magic kitten,' she gushed.

'Weee-ow,' the creature wailed again.

'You're doing it all wrong,' Ray sang.

'Yeah stew-pit,' Maggie said. 'You're supposed to drown it, not teach it to swim.'

'Shut up,' Frankie said, and slapped the bucket into the tub for another try.

'I know why it's not working,' Ray said smugly.

This time the kitten came up looking fresh. It appeared to be recovering instead of dying. Its big hazel eyes stared up at Frankie. Even Maggie was rooting for it now.

'Maybe we should let it go.'

'Yeah,' Dawn said.

Frankie shook his head. This was more than a simple mercy killing now: it was a test of manhood.

'How does it feel to be made a monkey of by a kitten?' Maggie gloated.

'I can tell you what you're doing wro-ong,' Ray sing-songed again.

'Close your stupid traps.'

When the kitten failed to drown a fifth and a sixth time, Frankie gave up. He decided to find out what his brother had to say.

'No good asking me now—you didn't want to know when you had the chance.'

Frankie grabbed Ray by the hair and pushed his face into the tub until his nose was within an inch of the water.

'OK, OK, you win.'

Frankie let him go.

'Doing it your way just traps the air in the bucket for the kitten to breathe. You have to tilt the bucket to one side so the water can get in.'

'Aw, flip it,' Dawn said. 'Why did you have to tell him?'

Frankie followed Ray's instructions. He felt the air shoosh-ing out between his fingers as he pressed the bucket down. Nobody said a word. They watched until the last air bubble had popped on the surface and the water had become still.

After a few minutes, Frankie slowly pulled the bucket out. There was a loud sucking squelch as it came clear. The soaked bedraggled body tumbled out onto the grass with a soft thunk. Clouds crossed in front of the sun. A sharp wind struck up, flapping Maggie's kaftan like a sheet. Suddenly, it turned cold.

'Hmmmph,' Maggie said and went in.

Now that it was over, Frankie was shocked. He folded the towel around the tiny body and stood up. Dawn broke into low sobs. Everyone shuffled their feet. Ray patted his little sister on the head.

'It's all right,' he cooed reassuringly, 'the kitten is in a far better place now.'

'Where?'

'Err... heaven.'

'Cats don't have heaven.'

'Right then, it's in fucking catland, OK?' Ray yelled and walked away in disgust.

Frankie brought the bundle to the sandpit at the foot of the back wall. Reverently, he deposited it on the sand. A sudden noise made him glance across at next door. Mary Figgis and her brother Harold were staring across the wall at him through thick round spectacles. Frankie gave them the finger but they kept staring.

'Murderer,' Dawn said softly and walked away.

Stunned and ashamed and alone, Frankie dug a hole in the sand with the plastic shovel and buried the dead kitten, towel and all.

A couple of mornings later, Frankie decided to run away again. He was sick of being abused for having no summer job, no money and even no steady girlfriend. Most of all, though, he deeply resented being pointed out to people as the guy who had murdered Buster's prettiest kitten. Dawn had embarrassed him further by telling everyone that the kitten had come back to life as soon as Frankie had left and had clawed its way out of the sandpit. It was now living wild in the back bushes and attacked anyone who came near it. Dawn said it was only waiting for a chance to scratch Frankie's face off.

Frankie phoned his friend Davy Dudley and asked if he wanted to run away with him. 'OK, I'll go,' Davy said after some thought, 'but I have to get back on Saturday for the big party in Stony Rogers' place.'

They caught a bus to the North Wall and decided to sneak aboard the ferry to Scotland.

'This'll be a doddle, wait and see,' Davy said with one of his toothy grins.

A ship steward caught them hiding behind a funnel and turned them over to the police. Two sergeants interviewed them for an hour, then called their parents. The runaways were brought home in a squad car.

Da met Frankie on the porch, led him into the study and locked the door. Then he clouted him across the face with an open palm, the same way the Christian Brothers had done at school.

After that, Da sat Frankie down in the old leather armchair and gave him a cigarette.

'Just answer me one question,' he said. 'Why Scotland?'

Afterwards, Frankie gave up running away. It wasn't really worth it, he decided, unless you had a place to run to.

6
DA

Da interrupted his morning wash to sneak up on his family with handfuls of shaving cream. He ambushed Frankie in the hallway. Then he splattered Maggie by the kitchen stove. Parnell got his on the porch. Soon, everyone was going around with bits of shaving cream stuck to their hair and clothes.

'Now, squoodlums, that'll show you who's master in this house,' Da said.

Da was leaving for New York to take part in a big new film. He would be gone for the whole summer. Frankie could not remember a summer when Da had not been away working on a film or a play. Ma was grumpy and sullen about it, but Dawn thought it was wonderful that her father was going to be in a movie.

'My daddy's going to be famous like John Travolta,' she chirped.

'John who...?' Ma asked.

As soon as Ma had cleaned the foam off her face, she scurried about helping to pack suitcases and tidy the house.

Frankie and Maggie and Dawn scurried about too. They wanted to show Da that he could rely on them to take care of things while he was away. They also wanted to make sure he sent them letters with lots of dollars in them. Everyone helped with the tidying and packing except Ray who retired to his room saying that he felt a novel coming on. He did not wish to be disturbed until Da was ready to go, he warned.

'That's not fair,' Maggie complained. 'He gets to rest while we work.'

'Leave Ray alone,' Ma said. 'He's a genius and geniuses need plenty of time on their own.'

Next came the farewell breakfast. Da ate a big plateful of eggs and rashers in the study. Ma and Maggie loitered by his chair in case he wanted anything else.

When he had finished, Da leaned out of the study into the hall where Frankie was dragging a rubbish bag. 'Call the squiggles,' he said.

Everyone assembled in the study, except Noelie who was happily walking the back wall. Da stood in front of the window. With his black greatcoat draped over his arm, he blocked out the sunlight, the pale blue sky, the fast-moving puffy clouds and the shimmering green sea beyond. He even deadened the billowy wind that was beating off the glass like snow. Frankie and Maggie stood by the fireplace. Da stared at a spot on the far wall while he made up his speech. Dawn sat on the black leather armchair, sucking on an apple and swinging her bare legs. Ma stood in the doorway. Her eyes were teary and wide and she looked as though she were about to burst out crying. But she stood there and took it for the sake of the kids. Ray came in and slouched over by the bookcases at the opposite end of the room, away from Frankie who had annoyed him this morning by taunting him that his 'old cowboy books were brutal'. Frankie grinned a big grin at his younger brother just to drive him crazy.

Da had on his best navy suit and a matching dark waistcoat with fancy silver buttons. As he cleared his throat and fixed his kids in the gaze of his large pale blue eyes, he fiddled with a paisley cravat which was tucked inside the neck of his special going-away grey shirt. His long straggly blond hair was tied behind in a ponytail. He shifted position and the day came flooding back into the room. Light flared across Da's head and streams of pink ran down the chinks in his wide craggy face. Frankie thought he looked like a granite statue coming to life.

'Children,' he began, then clasped his hands. 'I'll be away until September. It's up to you to look after your mother and mind the house. I don't want to hear about any of you acting the maggot.'

Da's head swivelled slowly to fix a pale gaze on his eldest. Frankie always felt like a kid when Da did that. He was seventeen going on eighteen. It was time he was treated as an adult.

Da raised an eyebrow. 'And I want you to get a summer job,' he said.

'But, Da I...'

'No buts. And no smart remarks either. You're very quick at changing the subject by making a joke. You have to earn your fees for university next year. Your mother and I don't have money growing out of our ears.'

Frankie frowned and looked down at the floor. He studied the toes of his runners. He heard Maggie sniggering. Whenever Da gave out to him sarcastically, Frankie felt lower than a dog. It reminded him of his humiliation one cold day the previous January when Da had walked into his bedroom to find him stretched on the bed playing with the toy soldiers he had bought secretly with the fiver Auntie Lucy had sent him for Christmas. Da had given him one of his stares, snorted 'Bit old for that now, aren't we?', then left as silently as he had come in. Frankie had felt so ashamed that he had immediately gathered up the soldiers, marched out the back and dumped them into the bin. He had been planning to give up playing with soldiers this summer anyhow. Another few months wouldn't have made any difference.

Da's lecture also reminded him that at the end of the summer the postman would deliver a long, white envelope containing his exam results. If he failed, there would be murder. Every time he thought about it he grew more certain that he was going to fail He was now convinced that he would require a massive stroke of luck just to pass—getting into university would take a miracle.

But there was no point thinking about it, he decided; from now on, he was going to put all thought of exam results and college out of his head until the end of the summer. Instead he thought about football and black leather jackets and the words of the new Stranglers' single.

Da told everyone to look after Noelie. He said that it wasn't Noelie's fault that he was the way he was. It was nobody's fault. They should all be particularly kind and understanding and give every support to their mother who had enough to put up with, God knows. Then he took a wad of green bills out of his pocket and stuffed it high on the bookshelf.

'Now feck off, the lot of you,' he said and dismissed them with a dramatic wave of his hand.

They left quietly so that Ma and Da could be alone. As he was going out of the door Frankie saw Ma fold into Da's big arms like an empty dress. Da stroked her long red hair with his large bony white hand. Ma burbled something into his chest.

'Ah now,' Da murmured, 'now...shish...shish...'

After Da had left, Ma sent Dawn up to the Summit for two Guinness and twenty Carrolls. Then she withdrew to the kitchen. She didn't even come out when Noelie threw a stone through Mr Figgis's greenhouse window. Then she refused to open the door when Frankie told her that Mr Figgis had threatened to call the police if Noelie didn't get down from his garden wall.

'Take Noelie for a long walk,' she shouted from behind the door.

So Frankie took Noelie by the hand and walked him up to the Summit shops. They bought ice-pops. The bored shop-girl had to move fast to stop Noelie taking a handful of chocolate bars from the display counter.

'Ah-ah,' she said.

'Ah-ah,' Noelie mimicked, and immediately tried for one of the sweet jars.

Outside, it was a bright, blowy day. There was a crowd sitting around on the wooden benches outside the pub, drinking beers and shorts and coloured minerals in tall glasses as they looked out at the view. Noelie said 'hello' to everyone he passed. Seconds later, in the same cheery voice, he told them to 'fuck off'. People just looked at him. Some girls tittered. An old man said 'hello' back.

Noelie didn't mind; he had a big orange ice-pop to suck and make slurping noises with, and a can of Heinz beans in his hand to show people. He had his big brother by the hand and he was going for a long walk.

They walked past the pub and turned the corner leading to the Summit view, the car parks and the cliff walks. While

Noelie sucked his ice-pop, Frankie gripped his brother's elbow and gently steered him out of the paths of others.

At the top of the hill, a long line of cars was drawn up in a neat row in the public viewing area. Noelie walked along the low wall and waved and said 'hello' to the sightseers in every car he passed. It was wild and green and windy. People sitting on the grass were buffeted like palm trees in a hurricane. But the wind didn't bother Noelie; he walked and waved and shouted greetings, laughed and scratched himself, tripped and righted himself without breaking stride.

At the end of the wall, Noelie presented his licked-clean ice-pop stick to a plump old lady in a grey overcoat who was looking out at the sea.

'Why, thank you,' the old lady said and smiled graciously.

Then, she walked away slowly with the ice-pop stick in her hand.

'He's a fine big fellow,' she called back against the breeze, 'what age is he?'

'Six,' Frankie answered without thinking—Noelie had been 'six' for nearly four years. 'No, he's ten,' Frankie yelled but the wind was howling and the lady had gone out of earshot. 'Ten,' Frankie roared anyway.

From the wall, Frankie could see the rolls of greenery winding down to the cliffs and the white-capped blueness. The only break in the wilderness was the creamy cone of the cliff lighthouse, rising up like a sentry from its slice of grey rock. The wind from the sea rocked him as he stood looking. It forced him to squint. But he could make out the lighthouse-keeper's house in the row of cottages at the far side of the bridge which joined the rock to the mainland.

Once, during a winter storm, a postman had been plucked off the bridge and blown out to sea, bicycle and all. Next day, they had found the postman's cap and a letter addressed to the lighthouse-keeper, nothing else. It was a story everyone on the hill had known for years. Like the one about the party of schoolboys who had disappeared while searching for birds' nests along the cliffs. Or the tale about the drunken hardman who had gone down to the pier one night to drink beer and had fallen between a fishing boat and the harbour wall; when they had dragged him out next day, his blue hands had been clutching a six-pack.

Nelson loved to tell the story about the two Hare Krishnas who had gone swimming off the east pier one gentle June morning, never to be seen again. Nelson said it was a sure sign that God wasn't too gone on Hare Krishnas.

In the midst of Frankie's recollections, something silver streaked through the air and narrowly missed the heads of a group of camera-toting Americans.

'Saaaay,' a big, purple-faced man in a billowing anorak shouted as he ducked.

The can of beans landed in the grass with a thud.

'Hello,' Noelie said warmly as he got down from the wall and retrieved his can. The American tourists stood and watched him, expecting him to throw it again at any second. 'Fuck off,' Noelie said with a smile and the tourists gasped.

Frankie jumped across the wall and grabbed Noelie by the hand. He escorted his brother off along one of the cliff paths before the tourists could recover from their shock.

'Hey, that's just great, buddy,' a large yellow-haired woman called after him, 'real nice country ya got here.'

When they got back, Ma was at the garden wall yelling at Mr Figgis. Dawn stood at her side holding her hand and looking up at the arguing adults with big innocent eyes. Ray was watching from the porch, practising his John Wayne stance. He gave Frankie a big wink.

'How dare you order my child down from her own family wall. This is our wall and my children have every right to walk along it whenever they wish.'

Mr Figgis was a tall confident man with thick black hair that flopped down over his left eye. He began setting out his grievances in a nasal English accent. He smiled to show that he was a reasonable man.

That was a big mistake.

'Don't smile at me, mister—I'm not your mammy.' Ma glared and took a pull on her cigarette. She blew the smoke in Mr Figgis's direction. 'You have no right to order Dawn down from her own garden wall.'

'I'm not ordering anyone. All I'm saying is that my wife and family deserve a little privacy. One of your children has already broken a window in my greenhouse and now the little girl is walking the wall making faces and rude gestures at my children. Surely you can see my point of view.'

Ma shrugged. 'Imagine that,' she said. 'Well, these are Griffin children. They're thoroughbreds. Pure Irish blood, descended from the High Kings of Tara. You'll never understand that. They can walk their 'Celtic' wall any time they want, day or night. This is our land. We're a free people now, no thanks to the likes of you.'

She gathered Dawn and Noelie and Ray to her and stood with her head high and her long red hair blowing in the wind like a warrior queen.

Mr Figgis attempted to make a few reasonable points. He explained that it had all been a misunderstanding. He hadn't ordered Dawn down from her wall at all, merely requested politely that she refrain from spying on his family while they were at lunch.

'Spying, my God, spying is it?'

'Well, I only meant...'

Oh yes, that's a good one all right—the English accusing the Irish of spying. Well, this is one family ye'll never conquer ye West Brit *bloodsucker*.'

Shocked, Mr Figgis took a step back. For a moment, he seemed to think that Ma was about to leap the wall and come at him. Then he shrugged off the thought and smiled to show that he forgave Ma's outrageous statements.

'Madam, I believe you're under a misconception...' he began.

'Mister, you *are* a misconception,' Ma said.

Then she threw her cigarette at him.

It was like slow-motion in a movie, Frankie thought. The cigarette bobbed gracelessly through the air like a runaway rocket, trailing a thin wisp of smoke; then ash fell away as its tip flared pink; halfway there, it appeared to swerve in order to pick its spot; finally, it struck Mr Figgis on the cheek with a splash of sparks, then dropped like a nail.

Mr Figgis looked at Ma in horror. Then he looked at the cigarette on the ground at his feet. He touched the black smudge on his cheek where the missile had hit.

He opened his mouth to say something, then changed his mind and walked away.

Ma twirled with a triumphant smile. She slapped her hands together like a child who'd just been awarded a prize. Frankie stared at her in shock. Even Noelie was struck dumb.

'You should be honoured to have Griffins walking this wall,' Ma shouted after Mr Figgis. 'Who cares about your old greenhouse anyway?'

As soon as Mr Figgis had slammed his front door, Ma ordered her children to get up on the wall.

'Aw God, Ma...' Frankie said.

Ma shushed him with an imperious flick of the wrist. 'This is our wall and we're going to walk it.'

She made Frankie cup his hands to give her a hoosh up onto the wall. Once up, she wobbled defiantly in her high heels until the others had joined her.

'Now, children,' she said, and started off along the wall towards the back garden. Frankie and Ray and Dawn and Noelie skittered after her like penguins across a wet plank. Parnell ran along the ground, barking.

They passed their neighbours' kitchen window. Inside, Mr Figgis and his wife and their bespectacled daughter Mary and horn-rimmed son Harold looked up in astonishment as the Griffin family paraded past along the wall.

'Hello,' Noelie said cheerfully and gave them a big wave. 'Fuck off.'

7

BULBS

First Nelson got a job on the fishing boats. Then Hopper got work in his Uncle Bill's butcher's shop. After that, Davy Dudley got taken on as an apprentice electrician. Finally, Frankie decided it was time to get his own act together. Ma helped him concentrate; she told him she would confiscate every dollar Da sent him from New York if he didn't get himself a summer job by the next Monday.

After a week of making grovelling phone calls, writing obsequious letters and trudging around the town's businesses meekly enquiring if there was any work going, Frankie got hired as a bulb-picker on Buller McGrath's farm. Bulb-picker had a nice ring to it. It sounded much grander than fisherman or butcher's assistant or apprentice electrician. He wasn't sure what a bulb-picker did exactly, but it paid thirty quid a week and that was good enough for him.

'Nobody in this house takes a slave job,' Ma exclaimed, tossing her hair back and giving him a fierce look.

'But you told me to get a summer job.'

'Yes, but not with that proddie landlord. I'll ring Commandant McDermott of McKee Barracks tomorrow and get you a proper job.'

'Aw, Ma...'

'Griffins are thoroughbreds. They don't work in fields.'

'They have to work somewhere, or else they don't get paid.'

Ma's eyes blazed. She gave a twisted, ironical smile. 'Oho, yes, very smart, aren't you? Just get out of my sight. Now, if you please.'

Ma was in a bad mood because Maggie had gone to Clare camping with her new boyfriend, Pierre Colcannon. It had been three days now and there was still no word from her. Ma had spent the morning phoning all the post offices in County Clare and leaving messages for Maggie to contact home immediately. In the end, that had just put her in an even worse humour.

Ma blamed Frankie; she said he was always off boozing with Nelson Fitzgerald and that Hopper fella or that ugly-looking punk rocker Davy Dudley who had a face like a horse when he could have been helping out around the place like cleaning the bathroom which was something he'd never dream of doing in a million years oh no because he was bloody well spoiled rotten or sweeping out the yard which even a monkey could see needed sweeping or hanging the washing on the line like a dutiful son instead of a dirty-haired layabout—did he think his shirts and trousers got washed by magic then marched up the back and threw themselves on the line?—or peeling the spuds for the dinner God knows the effort wouldn't break his arm or he could at least have taken Noelie for a long walk to ease the pressure on his mother's poor aching head which was splitting open trying to rear a large family all by herself without a bit of help from anyone except Ray who was the only one of them with any compassion.

'I should have had you adopted,' she proclaimed suddenly, following him into the hall and down the corridor to his room, 'then I wouldn't have all this worry. I was just too soft to use the wooden spoon on your backsides when you were growing up.'

Frankie said nothing. He closed the door of his room and waited until Ma gave up jabbering about his bad habits and shuffled back down the corridor to the kitchen. He felt like a rat. All he had done was to get himself a summer job and now somehow he was solely responsible for making his sister run off to County Clare with her new bloke. It made him go numb thinking about it. So he stopped thinking about it. At the end of the summer, he'd head for the US; he was sure this sort of thing never happened in California.

In the morning, though, things were better. Ma got up early, made him a big breakfast of scrambled eggs and toast and wished him the best of luck in his new job. She didn't say anything about slaves or proddie landlords. She didn't mention Commandant McDermott of McKee Barracks. Frankie felt pretty good walking down the hill to Buller McGrath's. At last, he would have his own money at weekends. It would be a relief not to have to beg from Ma or Nelson or any of the others. This weekend he would go into the city to the Dandelion Green and buy himself some punk badges and that new Ramones album. Perhaps he would ask Romy Casey out.

Then he found out what bulb-picking was.

His job was to crawl behind a hideously fuming tractor and pick bulbs out of newly ploughed furrows. The trick was to get the entire row's bulbs into a large wicker basket before the tractor came around again. He didn't have time to catch his breath before he had to start on another row. Then another. After half an hour he was so racked with pain he could scarcely breathe. He was very slow and the tractor had to keep stopping behind him. The driver yelled at him to get a move on. Sometimes he felt the plough tips trembling against his backside.

At the lunch break, the tractor driver—a fat, sweaty, red-faced man with a drooping black moustache—climbed down from his cab and beckoned Frankie to him. 'You're a long, streaky, useless, pox-bitten giraffe. I just thought you'd want to know.'

Frankie nodded. Then he walked away to a quiet corner and collapsed. After the break it was even tougher. At the end of the day Frankie tried to stand up but kept slumping forward into the muck. Another bulb-picker—a frog-faced boy with a thick Afro hairstyle—had to help him to the gate.

'By the way,' Frankie wheezed, 'what are these bulbs we're picking, anyhow?'

'Who gives a shite?' Frogface said. 'All I know is I get thirty quid a week to put 'em in baskets.'

'Er, thanks,' Frankie said.

'You're better off not knowing, believe me. It'll only interfere with your work.'

It was six days and nights before Maggie phoned, and then it was to say that she was on her way home. She'd be back in time for tea, she said—as long as Pierre's bike didn't break down. 'My God,' Ma said when she put the phone down, 'my sixteen-year-old daughter was driving around the country on the back of a motorbike. *I'll kill her.*'

Frankie and Ray exchanged glances.

'That Pierre's a bit of a lad all right,' Ray said.

'I heard he has six girlfriends,' Frankie said.

'Those ex-priests are always the worst.'

'He's got a nice moustache, though.'

'Yeah, his da gave it to him for his birthday.'

'Ah, he's not so bad.'

'No, he's been very well behaved ever since they let him out.'

'Think they'll get married?'

'Depends. They'll probably live together first.'

Ma whirled and pointed a fork at them. 'Shut up, the pair of ye, it's no joking matter.'

At teatime, Ma stiffened when she heard the roar of the motorbike coming up the driveway. She dropped a spoon into the sink, where it clanged about. Frankie and Ray kept their heads down and tried not to grin at each other.

When Maggie breezed into the kitchen a few minutes later as though nothing was wrong, Ma was just taking the hot plates of bacon and eggs from the cooker. A tall, bearded hippy loped in shyly behind, holding a crash helmet. Ma's face was tight and her mouth was twisted. She didn't turn around.

'Hi,' Maggie said gaily, coyly fondling her blonde curls, 'this is Pierre. Pierre, this is my family.'

'Er, hi,' Pierre said brightly. 'I've heard a lot about you.'

A plate of bacon and eggs hissed past their heads and splattered against the wall. Maggie and Pierre ducked and looked stunned. Ma plonked herself in front of them and pointed her finger at Maggie like a gun.

'How dare you. Nobody carries on like a tart in this house. Next time I let you out of my sight, it'll be over my dead body.'

'But Mammy...'

'Don't "Mammy" me, missy. You're cute enough with the "Mammys" when you want to be. Now you've disgraced the family in front of everyone on the road and mortified your father over in America.'

Maggie started to shout back, but Pierre motioned for her to stop. He put out his hands and assumed a sincere expression.

'I can assure you, Mrs Griffin, absolutely nothing happened. I have only the best of intentions towards your daughter.'

'Yes, just what are your intentions, mister? Do you intend to marry my daughter?'

Pierre's sincere expression fell off. 'I...em...well...' he began.

'Do you or don't you?'

'Well not this very minute,' Pierre said and laughed as if it were all a big joke. He looked around and saw that nobody else was smiling. He cleared his throat and put on a serious face. 'Er, I suppose we could always live together for a bit first, y'know, to see how we get on...'

There was a moment's silence. Everyone looked at Ma.

'Right,' Ma said and grabbed Pierre by the throat. She began hauling him out of the room. 'Uuuugh,' Pierre spluttered as he was dragged out of the kitchen and through the hall with Maggie holding on to his arm and Ma yelling into his ear at the top of her voice: '*Who do you think you are that you can kidnap my daughter?*'

'I'm sure we can discuss this,' Pierre roared before Ma opened the front door and pushed him out.

'Get out of my house. I wouldn't let my daughter marry you now even if she was pregnant with triplets.'

Maggie burst into tears and stormed into her room, banging the door. 'That's the last time I ever bring a friend back to this kip!' she yelled. 'Tomorrow I'm going away for good. I never want to see any of you again!'

'Good riddance to bad rubbish!' Ma shouted and marched into the study. The door of the study banged to. From outside came the rattle of a motorbike starting up.

Ray looked around and surveyed the broken china and the bits of egg and bacon scattered about the kitchen.

'Not bad for the first visit. I think Ma likes him.'

Hours later, Frankie was in the study watching *Top of the Pops* when Ma pulled up a chair beside him. She fidgeted for a while, looking at the TV screen but seeing nothing.

'She's got to learn—it's for her own good.'

'Yes Ma.'

'I'm a good mother. I'm not unfair.'

'No, you're not.'

'Maybe I was a bit too hard.'

'Maybe just a bit.'

'He seemed like a nice boy.'

'Well, he had a nice moustache.'

Ma stood up suddenly with a tense, determined expression and padded out into the hall. A few moments later, Frankie heard a soft rapping on Maggie's door. The door creaked open. There were urgent whisperings and shufflings, then gushing, breathless explanations followed by a general outbreak of sobbing and mutual declarations of love. Finally, Ma told Maggie in a loud tearful voice that she was the best of them all and could bring her new boyfriend to tea tomorrow or the next day or any day she wanted.

Frankie was so disgusted he switched off the TV and went for a walk up the back garden to cool off. Compared to this, he reckoned, bulb-picking was a picnic.

At midnight the phone rang and woke everyone up. Ma ran down the hall to the study in her dressing gown and grabbed the receiver. From their bedroom at the bottom of the corridor, Frankie and Ray could tell it was Da by the way Ma's voice went soft and gooey. They rose silently and gathered in the study. Maggie came in too. She stood palely sniffling by the door, a big red nose on her from all the crying earlier.

Everything was fine over here, Ma told Da; oh yes, the children were behaving themselves and the letters with the money in them had arrived and no, there were no problems with electricity bills or anything like that.

After talking for a while, Ma gave the phone to each of her kids in turn. Frankie told Da that he was a bulb-picker now and Da said that that was good and he was sending him something in the post. Ray came next and said that he'd read an Ian Fleming book and was going to write one that was better now that he could see how it was done—he wanted to know if it was true that you could rollerskate on the footpaths in New York without getting arrested and Da said that he hadn't seen any skaters but that he'd be sure to look out for them. Ma got Dawn up and put her on and Dawn said sleepily that she'd like Da to bring her back a Barbie Doll and maybe a Barbie Doll's house and Da promised he would. Finally, with a smile, Ma handed the phone to Maggie. Maggie took it and smiled back.

Everything's grand here,' she said. 'How're things over there?'

Later, Frankie dreamed he was up in the attic with Clara. Clara lit a candle and they sat at a small table by the window. She listened as he poured out his problems. He told her he was fed up with Ma giving out about his hair and his manners all the time and how he really hated it when Maggie left his records out of their sleeves, lying all over the floor to be walked on, and the way he always felt guilty whenever Ray got smart with him and he ended up having to box him one. He explained how he tried very hard to stay out of trouble around the house but that trouble just seemed to happen to him anyway, no matter what. Now he didn't know where his life was going any more. Why didn't everyone just give him a break? You'd think he was an axe-murderer the way some of his family carried on about him. Nothing ever seemed to go right for him. Bulb-picking was just another lousy part of the lousy summer he was having. Every morning when he looked at those rows and rows of bulbs, he felt like screaming. He'd be lucky if he could still walk at the end of the picking season.

Clara nodded sympathetically and smiled. It seemed strange to be opening his heart to his older sister, but it made him feel good. Sometimes he thought that Clara was the only one in the world who truly understood him. She always had time to listen, always seemed to know exactly what he meant. Whenever he talked to her he felt sure that everything was going to work out all right in the end.

Clara handed him an apple and he said 'thanks' and bit into it. They sat and looked out of the window in silence while Frankie chewed. They watched the first skinny orange fingers of dawn snaking over the horizon. He leaned back in his chair and stretched and smiled across at his sister. Clara handed him another apple. 'Someday I'm going to do something great,' he said. 'I'll write a book or make a film or become a famous rock singer.' Clara said she had no doubt about it. She told him he was a High King, with royal blood in his veins. They sat by the window, munching apples and looking out at the hill as the morning took hold.

When it was time to go, Clara stood up and softly blew out the candle flame. Frankie said 'goodbye,' opened the window and climbed out onto the narrow ledge. Then he floated down to the porch like a kite. Before going in, he looked up at the attic window and waved. Clara waved back, then pulled the window shut.

8
ERIN

There was a banshee in the kitchen.

It was perched on a high stool by the window, smoke gushing from its mouth. Frankie watched from the doorway as hazy sunshine flooded the room like spotlights and glistened along the creature's long crinkly seaweed hair. The banshee took on colours, shimmered, began to levitate...any second now its mouth would open and a horrible wailing sound would start.

Suddenly the banshee tossed a peeled spud into the sink, took the cigarette out of its mouth and turned around. 'Stop standing there like a bloody gom and call the rest of them,' it said.

When everyone had been gathered, Ma announced in a cracked voice that an American visitor was arriving next morning from Milwaukee. This visitor was the daughter of a prominent Irish-American Republican friend of the family; she was seventeen and her name was Erin.

'Her name is what?' everyone said.

'What's wrong with Erin? It's a fine Celtic name.' Ma told them that Da had sent word from America that everyone should be nice to Erin—anyone who acted the maggot could forget all about any more letters from New York with dollars in them. In particular, Da wanted Frankie to give up his free weekends in order to show their guest around.

'Aw God, Ma...' Frankie protested, but Ma cut him short.

'If that's the way your father wants it, then that's the way it's going to be.'

Erin's father, Ma added, owned a big cinema in downtown Milwaukee.

'Betcha it shows porno movies,' Ray joked. Ma told him to leave the room.

'What's a porno movie?' Dawn asked.

'You get out, too.'

Ma lit another cigarette and went back to her potato peeling.

'You don't deserve a mother like me, none of you do.'

Erin arrived by taxi at eight next morning. She was small and frumpy with a round, pleasant face and curly brown hair that flowed all the way down to her ankles. She wore flared jeans and a white blouse that had flowers on it. By her side was a tiny replica of herself. The only difference was that the replica wore a big pout.

'God, they're hippies,' Frankie whispered.

'Look who's talking,' Maggie said. 'Sure, your hair's so long you can't see your own two feet.'

'Well, hi!' Erin cried with a big toothy grin.

Ma welcomed them and gave them big hugs. 'You're both very welcome to your own Celtic homeland. *Céad míle Fáilte Roimh*—may you live long and prosper and may you have children and grandchildren and grandchildren's grandchildren by the multitude.'

'Oh, that's so nice. Thank you,' Erin beamed. Frankie and Ray and Maggie said 'hello'. Dawn just watched.

'This is my sister, Rainbow,' Erin said, indicating the sulky kid at her side. 'She's thirteen. I don't know if Pop wrote you but she's decided to come along. Say "hi", Rainy.'

Rainy said 'hi' without breaking into a smile or shifting her gaze from the milk bottles on the doorstep.

Ma ushered them inside and Frankie and Ray brought in the suitcases. In the kitchen, Ma poured out the tea while Erin gushed over each of them in turn. She started with Ray who didn't mind being gushed over one bit. 'What a cute smile you've got there,' Erin said, and Ray blushed. Maggie shook hands but refused to let her hair be mussed. Dawn didn't shake hands because she was locked in a staring contest with Rainbow. 'It's so wonderful to be here in Ireland, I can't tell you. I feel as though I have known each of you for years.'

'Does your Daddy show porno movies?' Dawn asked suddenly.

'Well, I err... I don't think so. I... what a strange question...' Erin began but Ma told her not to mind Dawn, that she was only six and had a peculiar outlook on life.

When Erin came to Frankie, her face broke into an expression of deepest ecstasy. 'Oh, just like your pop said— a real handsome Irish prince.'

Ray and Maggie broke into fits of giggles as Frankie glared.

'Now, what would you like for breakfast, Rainbow?' Ma asked. 'How about a great big plate of Irish sausages and rashers?'

'I just wanna go to the toilet,' Rainbow said.

'Oh, but you must eat something after your long flight.'

'I don't give a fuck. I wanna piss.' Conversation ceased.

Everyone looked at Rainbow. Then they turned to Erin who smiled weakly.

'She's thirteen,' Erin explained.

Ray was despatched to show Rainbow where the toilet was.

'It must have been a *very* long flight', Ma said.

Frankie and Ray spent the day showing the visitors around the neighbourhood. Erin was euphoric about everything— fields, haystacks, the local shop, the green outside the Summit pub, the seagulls, and especially Parnell who kept jumping up to lick her face, which made her giggle.

Rainbow, though, remained sullen. Ray decided to cheer her up.

'Why did the glowworm feel embarrassed?' he asked her, breaking into his best showbiz smile.

Rainbow shrugged.

'Cos it spent ten minutes chatting up a cigarette end.'

'Big deal,' Rainbow said.

'OK, here's a good joke,' Ray said undaunted. 'A wife says to her husband, "Darling, have you got a good memory for faces?" and the husband says, "Yes, I have" and the wife says, "That's good because I've just dropped your shaving mirror".'

Rainbow scratched her nose. 'So what?' she said.

Ray's smile became strained. 'What's yellow and highly dangerous?' he said with desperation in his voice.

Rainbow said nothing.

'Shark-infested custard,' Ray explained with a triumphant grin. 'Get it?'

'Yeah, I get it all right and I wish you were in it,' Rainbow said and walked off.

Crushed, Ray went home to write a novel, leaving Frankie as tour guide. As they strolled along the leafy boreen to the town, Frankie tried to pump Erin for information on the States. He would need contacts when he got over there, he figured, so the smart thing was to find out all he could; perhaps her Pop would give him a job in his moviehouse, or maybe they knew a rock band that needed a new roadie.

'Oh, let's not talk about the boring old US. Tell me about Ireland. I wanna hear all about the Easter Rising of 1916... my Pop told us all about it but I wanna hear the Real McCoy—did the British burn down all of Dublin or just most of it?'

Frankie did his best but no matter what he said, Erin seemed to know a lot more about Ireland than he did. She rattled off the roll call of great Irish patriots as though reciting a list of her favourite rock stars. Frankie began to think that going to the States might not be such a brilliant idea after all.

At breakfast next morning, Erin was bright-eyed and chirpy and full of stories about Milwaukee and her Pop's cinema and all the great plays Frankie's Da had taken them to when they had visited him in New York the week before. She just loved music. 'My favourite band are Jethro Tull. They're just so spiritual.'

Frankie told her that he liked The Clash and The Ramones and The Stranglers.

'Oh, you shouldn't listen to that punk stuff—it's so full of negative values,' she warned.

After a while, Frankie noticed that Erin was gazing deeply into his eyes. It gave him a weird feeling. He became so unnerved he put two spoons of salt into his tea.

She insisted on walking him to work. All the way down the hill to Buller McGrath's farm, she chattered about how wonderful it was to be in her homeland at last and how lucky Frankie was to have such a great mother.

'She's like a queen, you know. They'd just adore her in Milwaukee. Everyone over here is so noble. Did I tell you that the cabbie who brought us from the airport was a cousin of James Joyce's? Isn't that *amazing*?'

At the lunch break, Erin descended on him with coffee and sandwiches. The other bulb-pickers were very impressed. Most were convinced Frankie had something really heavy going with her. The tractor driver climbed down from the cab, big red face beaming. It was the first time Frankie had ever seen him in a good mood.

He came over to Frankie. 'She's stimulatin',' he sleazed. 'Are ye buryin' the baldy fella, then?'

'She's the daughter of a friend of my Da's,' Frankie explained.

'Course she is, and I'm the Queen of Belgium.'

After work, Frankie took Erin for a stroll along the cliff top. They traipsed the rocky paths and back lanes and twisting descents and rises until Frankie thought his legs were going to explode. When they got home, Erin wasn't even short of breath; she told Ma it had been relaxing.

'I was in Big Sur last summer. Did you know the waves there sometimes come right up over the cliffs?' That evening, they went down to the harbour and watched the fishing boats going out. Erin cooed and said it was just mindblowing. Rainbow said the smell of fish made her want to throw up. Somehow Frankie managed to avoid Nelson and anyone else he knew.

On the walk home, Erin took Frankie's arm and talked about the beautiful sunrises she'd seen in California last summer.

'Don't tell me,' Frankie said, 'sometimes the sun comes right up over the cliffs.'

'Right, how did you know?' Erin asked in surprise.

On Wednesday Ma took everyone to the Abbey Theatre to see a Brendan Behan play. At the interval, Erin wanted to know what 'bolix' meant. Ma told her it was a religious term. It was sometimes used by Republicans when they got excited, Ray added.

When Frankie was at work, Ray and Maggie took it in turns to look after the visitors. One day they visited the National Museum, the next Maggie took them on a bus trip to Glendalough. In the evenings, they hung around the Summit. Erin thought the place was 'really quaint'.

'Yeah,' Rainbow said, 'like Hiroshima after they dropped the bomb.'

After a week, everyone except Ma and Frankie avoided Rainbow. Frankie would have given her a miss too, but he was determined to do his best to make the visit a success, even if it meant occasional humiliation. When Rainbow called him a 'droopy-looking scumbag' in front of Mrs Figgis from next door, he smiled and thought about envelopes packed with greenbacks.

It was becoming obvious that he was going to get no help from Maggie, Ray or Dawn. Whenever they saw Frankie with Erin and Rainbow returning from one of their 'excursions', they hightailed it up the back garden or disappeared over the side walls.

It got so bad that Frankie called an emergency general meeting in the garage.

'Erin's a pain,' he explained, 'but that Rainbow is like something out of *The Exorcist.*'

'She's just right for you so,' Maggie said, smirking.

'Ignore her,' Ray advised, 'the little demon is bound to calm down sooner or later.'

'I don't know how long I can stand it,' Frankie said, hoping that a rare display of vulnerability would swing them to his side.

'Tough shit. It couldn't happen to a nicer guy,' Maggie said and flounced off.

In the morning, Erin wanted Frankie to take her to Belfast. She said she felt a great need to 'relate' to 'the Troubles'.

'It's not much fun "relating" to an explosion,' Frankie explained, but Erin remained adamant.

'I wanna go too,' Rainbow chipped in. 'At least it's bound to be more fun than this dump.'

'OK, I'll take you up there if you take me to Vietnam so I can relate to the craters your bombers made,' Frankie snapped.

In the end, Ma came out against the trip; she said the situation up there was difficult enough without adding Rainbow. To make up for the disappointment, Ma told Frankie to take the girls into the city to go shopping.

Grafton Street had seemed a safe bet, but Rainbow hated everything: the clothes shops were 'backward'; she thought the ice-cream was 'yucky'; and every restaurant Frankie brought them to was 'sleazeball central'.

In desperation, Frankie took them to an American hamburger joint called 'Thunderbirds'.

'Call this a hamburger?' Rainbow shouted when she was handed her order of cheeseburger and french fries. Her voice cut through the Steely Dan song that was blaring from the overhead sound system. 'This is a fucking cow's abortion. If I eat this, I'll be barfing for a month.'

Everyone in the place stopped eating. Some began examining their own burgers. The waitress snatched Rainbow's plate away. The manager came across and asked them to leave.

Outside, Frankie controlled himself with great effort and explained to Rainbow that she was being unreasonable as well as rude and bad-mannered and arrogant; if she didn't like it here, she could call her father as soon as they got home and make arrangements to go back to America.

For the first time since she had arrived in the country, Rainbow smiled. It was a warm smile—happy, carefree, revealing a set of perfect white teeth. It put Frankie at ease, and made Erin smile too.

'Say what you want, motherfucker. I'm going for a fucking coke,' Rainbow said and strode off without looking behind to see if they were following.

Next evening, as soon as tea was over, Ma decided that everyone should do party pieces. They sat at the kitchen table and watched as Ray narrowed his eyes, hitched up an imaginary gunbelt and turned into John Wayne. He swaggered slowly across to Erin. 'Yew'll drink yer milk 'cos it's good fer ya,' he drawled and everyone laughed.

'Oh, that's so good,' Erin squealed.

'Huh,' Rainbow said, but everyone ignored her.

Ma wanted Frankie to recite a poem by W. B. Yeats but Frankie refused.

'Don't "aw Ma" me, mister, do it for our guests.' Still Frankie shook his head. He could feel Erin's imploring gaze on him; when he looked up, her big round face was beaming in anticipation. Ma ordered him to recite but Frankie wouldn't budge.

'Coward,' Ma sneered and flapped her arms like a chicken; 'Bac-bac-bac-bac. All right, come on, Dawn, and sing us that song I taught you about the Easter Rising.'

Dawn hid under the table. Ma looked at Maggie but Maggie raised her eyes to heaven and went into a sulk.

'None of ye are any use except Ray. Here, I'll show ye how it's done.'

Ma got to her feet, took Ray by the hand and hauled him up too. Then she commenced to jig around the kitchen, keeping her back straight as a pole and. her arms stiff by her sides. Her red hair bounced up and down behind her as she sang: 'Diddle-ee-eye-dill, diddle-ee eye-dill, diddle-ee-eye-dill, eye-dill eye.' From time to time, she let out a whoop and stamped on the floor. Ray stopped dancing and put on his John Wayne face again but Ma stamped on his foot. John Wayne said 'ow' and resumed jigging. Erin and Dawn and Maggie clapped their hands in time and hollered as Ma and Ray jigged around the kitchen, giggling like children as they attempted to stamp on one another's toes.

As soon as the others jumped up and joined in, Frankie slid out of the door. He walked up and down the back garden with his head down and kicked at anything he saw in order to shake off the humiliation of being made to look like a fool in front of the Americans. He felt angry and hurt and fed up. Ma always treated him like an idiot or a child or a waster— and sometimes all three.

In a while, the rage and the shame went away and he began to feel numb instead. Soon he had calmed down enough to think about California. Soon he felt a whole lot better...until he remembered that California was full of Americans who could turn out to be just like Erin and Rainbow. That in turn reminded him of exams and exams reminded him of college and college made him think about America again and, in the end, the whole lot made him so depressed that he marched into the sandpit and kicked sand over the back wall until the singing and dancing noises from the house had faded completely.

Erin found him there afterwards. She walked up to him, flushed and delirious-looking. She looked so happy and healthy and optimistic she made Frankie sick.

'Gosh, your mom is a-may-zing, really. You never told me she was a direct descendant of the High Kings of Tara. You're a very lucky guy to have a mother who's an aristocrat.'

'Yep, I sure am,' Frankie said.

On Saturday morning, Frankie and Hopper and Nelson were invited to play for the Hill team in the big match against the town. Frankie knew that the Big Guys were desperate for players because Vinnie Cassidy—old Gaptooth himself—had personally asked him. They met that night at the Summit to talk tactics.

'Just do your best,' Vinnie told him, 'but make a balls of things and I'll fracture your skull.'

At home, Erin was disappointed that it was soccer. 'Why can't you play baseball?' she asked. 'Now that's what I call a real game.'

On the afternoon of the big match, Frankie and Nelson and Hopper arrived early outside the Summit bursting with enthusiasm, only to find the Big Guys already on the green passing a flagon of cider between them.

'Well, well, well,' Vinnie Cassidy sneered, 'if it isn't the Three Wise Men.'

The new arrivals had just put on their football boots when Jack the Rack shouted, 'Time for a warm-up.'

Vinnie Cassidy, Bobby Gallo and ugly bushy-haired Flow-erpower Dolan, Cyril McLean the lighthousekeeper's son and Jack himself charged across the road into the Summit pub leaving Frankie and Nelson and Hopper standing half changed on the green feeling like complete idiots. Hopper ran over for a look.

'I think it's gonna be an interesting match,' he said when he returned a few moments later. 'Jack's just bought a bottle of Southern Comfort.'

In a little while, Frankie clacked across the road in his boots and squinted through the brown-tinted window to see for himself. The Big Guys were clustered around the pool-table drinking and laughing and dancing about to Thin Lizzy who were blasting from the jukebox. As he watched, Jack the Rack stretched out on the counter and closed his eyes as he wailed along with the song, using the tip of a pool cue as a microphone:

'The Boys are Back in Town
The Boys are Back in Tow-ow-ow-ow-own.'

When the Townies arrived, Nelson went into the pub and told the Big Guys.

'Who cares?' Jack bellowed. 'We're gonna lash them out of it anyhow. What's the big rush?'

'They can fucken well find themselves another goalie,' Nelson said when he came out, and clattered off home in disgust without even bothering to change.

After waiting around for a time, the Townies sat down on the benches outside the pub and ordered pints. 'Fuck this for a game of cowboys,' the town captain said, and lit a joint.

Maggie and Ray with Erin and Rainbow showed up as the Big Guys were spilling out of the pub. Then Ma came along with Noelie by the hand. She pointed to Frankie, and Noelie shouted and waved and banged his can of beans on the bonnet of a parked Volkswagen. Erin was wearing a blue and grey striped cheerleader's outfit and waving a pair of frilly pom-poms at him. Frankie couldn't believe it. He tried to keep his dignity intact, but it slid away from him like a bar of soap across a bathroom floor.

'Yay, Frankie,' she cheered, 'Go, buddy, go.'

Jack the Rack swaggered on to the green and hitched his shorts up over his drooping beer-belly. He gathered the Big Guys in a circle for a pep talk. 'Fuck all this peace and love and understanding. Let's get out there and mangle them. I wanna be up to me nose in blood.' Before the kickoff, Vinnie Cassidy came up to Frankie wearing his most charming expression and took him to one side: 'Remember what I said, one wrong move and you're dead, OK?'

'Go, Frankie,' Erin shouted from the sideline.

'Frak, fuck off,' Noelie called and laughed, and everyone around laughed too.

'Pity you couldn't pick a good Irish game like hurling instead of this Brit propaganda,' Ma yelled with her face stern as a statue.

'Oh God,' Frankie said to Hopper. 'This is all I need.'

'The Yank's a bit of all right,' Hopper said. 'Tell us, are ye burying the baldy fella then?'

Right from the kickoff, players were knocked down whether they had the ball or not and shots were ballooned into the surrounding fields. Vinnie Cassidy played with a pint of Guinness in his hand; Jack the Rack kept his cigarette in his mouth. Whenever he tackled anyone there was an explosion of sparks. Flowerpower Dolan shot the ball into oncoming traffic and snapped the wing mirror clean off a new Ford Escort which then skidded into the kerb. The driver got out and shouted at Flowerpower, and Flowerpower shouted back and the game went on oblivious. Half the time, nobody seemed to know where the ball was. Hopper said it didn't matter as long as it was a good game. Just when things were settling down, two wild white horses from the far field galloped across the pitch.

'Gee,' Frankie heard Erin say to Ma, 'I've never come across anything like this. Are horses part of the game too?'

'Only when they can't get enough players,' Ma said. After twenty minutes, the Townies scored. None of the Big Guys could figure it out. One moment everyone was carrying on as usual, the next the ball was in the net and the Townies were jumping up and down. Goalkeeper Cyril McLean hadn't seen it either. He had been throwing up at the side when the shot was taken.

'Fucken fluke,' Jack the Rack snorted.

'A mere technicality,' Flowerpower Dolan said.

'It's all your fucken fault,' Vinnie Cassidy roared at Frankie.

'Fuck'n faut, fuck'n faut,' Noelie chimed merrily from the sideline.

A minute later, Frankie dribbled through the Townies' defence and passed the ball to Jack the Rack who was in the clear with only the town goalkeeper to beat, but Jack tripped over his own feet and collapsed in a heap. One of the Townies got the ball and started a run upfield.

Jack struggled to his feet with difficulty and put his hands on his hips. '*Penalty!*' he roared. '*I was bleedin' tripped!*'

There were loud arguments and much pointing and shouting and name-calling.

'Pen-al-ty. I was bleedin' tripped,' Jack repeated. The Townie captain said that it couldn't have been a penalty because Jack had tripped himself. Jack said he was going home for his hatchet. The Townie captain said that it probably was a penalty after all, now that he thought about it.

Everyone cleared the goal area. Jack took the ball and carefully measured ten paces from the goal-line to the spot from where he thought the penalty kick should be taken. As he ran up to shoot, the Townie goalkeeper clutched at himself and closed his eyes. Jack whacked the ball and fell down. The ball cannoned off the goalkeeper's head with a 'ker-ump' and soared directly upwards. Nobody had ever seen a football go so high.

'Goal!' Jack roared, raising his hands in the air like a champion and giving himself a running commentary as he ran back to his cheering teammates: 'Great fucken goal, just listen to that fucken crowd, *waaaaaa...*'

Vinnie Cassidy sent Frankie and Hopper to look for the ball. It took ten minutes to revive the town goalkeeper.

At half-time, the Townies were winning by twelve goals to one. Jack had retired to the sideline where he sat drinking a pint and discussing his wonderful penalty kick with anyone who happened to be nearby. Cyril McLean was stretched out on the goal-line, unable to move. Vinnie Cassidy blamed Frankie for the state of the Hill team. He told him to go into goal.

'No, why should I?'

'Because if you don't, I'll break your fucken face.'

Frankie had finally had enough of Vinnie's bullying. He was too old to be let himself be pushed around. 'Oh yeah,' he said, 'you and whose army?'

Vinnie loafed Frankie on the nose and Frankie staggered back.

There was a roar from the sideline: '*How dare you hit my son, you blackguard!*' Vinnie took one look and ran for it as Ma charged onto the pitch, fist upraised, with Erin and Maggie and Ray following.

'You...scumbag,' Erin shrilled.

As soon as he had recovered, Frankie took off in the opposite direction towards home. Hopper caught up with him at the entrance to his driveway.

'See, told you it was going to be an interesting' game,' he said.

Frankie knew something was up when Ma took him on one side and offered him a thousand pounds for a grandchild. 'Doesn't matter if it's a boy or a girl,' she enthused, 'as long as it's born in Ireland.'

Ma looked so young and happy and excited that he almost wished he happened to have a grandchild on him there and then.

Later, Erin handed him a carefully wrapped package. Inside was a copy of *Jonathan Livingston Seagull* by Richard Bach. The inscription read: 'To My Irish Prince—Francis Griffin'.

'Er, thanks.'

'You're welcome,' Erin said. 'It's a beautiful book. I'd really like to talk to you about it when you've finished it.'

Next morning, Frankie woke up to find a red rose on his pillow attached to a piece of white parchment which had blackened edges and hundreds of tiny 'I Love You's scrawled across it. Ray couldn't meet his eyes without smirking. Maggie called him 'lover boy'. He overheard Ma on the phone to Da in New York saying that the two young people were 'head over heels'. When Dawn asked him if she could visit him in

America sometime, he snapped that he'd lock her in the attic with Clara if he heard another word out of her. Dawn went pale and ran away. He decided it was time to take action.

After lunch, he took Erin for a stroll. He chose to take her along one of the remote trails. He didn't talk much. He wanted to be sure that what he had to say to her would be delivered with maximum impact. After all, she was a nice girl. He didn't want to hurt her. Erin was unusually quiet too. From time to time, she threw him a concerned, expectant look.

When they had reached a spot which was well hidden from the cliffs above and the pathways below, Frankie took Erin by the shoulders and turned her around to face him. Then he began to speak, but before he had the first word out, Erin's lips were on his. She forced him to the ground and they ended up rolling into a thicket of ferns, flattening it.

'Oh, Frankie,' Erin said from somewhere above him, 'I thought you were never going to do it. You're just so darned shy.'

Frankie tried to say something, but Erin was on him again. He found himself kissing her back without really wanting to. He couldn't move under her. She sat on his chest and her knees were on his arms, and his face was absolutely smothered by her long hair. For a moment, he was positive he was going to suffocate.

Next time Erin broke the kiss, he gathered all his breath and screamed.

'Oh, I'm sorry,' Erin said with a worried look, 'am I hurting you?'

He scrambled to his feet and ran as fast as he could.

Next evening, Frankie tried again. To play it safe and avoid a repeat of the grappling session, he confronted Erin and

Rainbow in the driveway as they returned from yet another stroll. He had intended to be diplomatic and gently explain to Erin that she had gone too far and was taking things a bit too seriously for her own good, but when he saw that she was making goo-goo eyes at him again, and when he suddenly remembered the amount of misery Rainbow had caused him over the past three weeks—particularly the time she had called him a 'scrawny, dog-faced numb-nuts' and made a show of him in front of Nelson and Hopper and all the Big Guys—he lost the run of himself.

He took a deep breath and told them at the top of his voice that they were obnoxious, insensitive, rude, stupid, greedy, bloody pathetic out-of-date hippie brats in love with themselves. He was embarrassed to be seen with them, he roared. He called them 'a pair of selfish little monsters'. In case they still didn't get the message, he threw in the religious term they'd heard at the Abbey Theatre that night. As a finale, he told them their American accents made them sound 'like a pair of fucking chipmunks'.

Then he stood wheezing for breath like an old bulldog.

Erin looked shocked. Rainbow had lost a little of her suntan. Frankie didn't care; he was glad he had finally got it all off his chest. At least now he wouldn't have to put up with any more crap. Suddenly, Erin came over and put her arms around him. He was so surprised he couldn't move.

'Oh, my poor Frankie,' she said softly. 'So much hurt and pain. So many wounds. It's good to get it all out of you. You don't have to worry any more. Cry if you want. I'm here now.'

He would have cried, but he didn't have the strength.

For the next few days, Frankie disappeared up the back garden and across the fields every time Erin and Rainbow came out of their room.

Erin finally got the message.

Frankie felt her sorrow-filled eyes on him at breakfast every morning. At tea, she pushed little notes across the table to him that he pretended not to see. Once, late at night, he heard her crying in her room.

Ma gave Frankie accusing looks.

'I don't want to marry her,' Frankie explained.

'Why not?' Ma exclaimed, wide-eyed. 'You should be glad that anyone would want to marry a long-haired fool like you.'

'I'm only seventeen,' he said in desperation.

'Big deal. What do you want—a medal?'

During the final week of the girls' visit, Frankie tried very hard to be polite. He still felt Erin's gaze on him at mealtimes and last thing at night. He spent a lot of time at Nelson's. Once in bed, he lay feeling like a murderer, unable to sleep.

Erin and Rainbow left for the airport at seven in the morning. As the taxi pulled away, they rolled down the windows and waved. Erin looked heartbroken, Rainbow seemed deliriously happy. Maggie and Ma, Dawn and Noelie and Ray waved back from the porch. Frankie waved too. He didn't feel relieved, as he had thought he would. Instead he felt guilty and a little sad. He kept getting the feeling he was missing something.

That night he flopped about in the bed like a loose mackerel on the deck of a fishing boat. In the morning, he awoke face down on the floor with his nose pressed into one of Ray's socks.

Two weeks later he got a letter:

Dear Frankie,

I'm sorry I came on a little too strong for you. I guess that's just the way us US kids are. Anyway, I just want you to know that I had a real good time in Ireland and I'll always be your friend. I didn't really want to marry you, as you obviously thought, though if you ask I'll definitely consider it. It's a pity we didn't have more time together to have fun and just talk, but I guess that's the way it is when you're on holiday in a strange country with a weird little sister to take care of. By the way, Rainy really misses you all and says that she really enjoyed your sermon on the driveway. She says you used some really cute words. It's never too late for miracles, huh?

I start college in a month so I'll write when I get myself organized. It's all so new to me that I don't know where I'm going or what I'm doing around the house anymore. Even my own room looks strange. Must be the Irish hangover.

In the meantime, take care of yourself and give my love to your magnificent 'Celtic' mom and the rest of your family. I'll always treasure the memories. It was really special. Say what you like but you'll always be my Irish Prince. You must come over here sometime. I know my family would love to meet you. I'd kinda like it too.

All my love,

Your Wife (whoops sorry) friend.

Erin XXXXXXX

P.S. I hope you don't think this letter is another come-on. If I don't hear from you, I'll just regard it as one of life's hard lessons. I'll say we were a pair of lost souls who passed each other in the night.

E.

9
DAVY

He is in bed in the back garden in the middle of a big storm. Wind howls in his ears like thousands of mad cats, and thunder cracks and starts every dog on the hill arooooing. Beside him, lightning dances on spindly legs, but he is not a bit scared: when he was small, Ma told him that thunder was just some angel beating on a big drum and, sure, lightning was only God the Son messing with a flashlight. Nothing to get worked up about. So, chin over the top blankets like a kid, he stares straight up into the twirling blackness. Flotillas of burst pillows charge about the sky and millions of gleaming stars wink down at him like shiny new marbles begging to be picked up and flicked at one another. A lop-sided half-moon creeps around a cloud like an old drunk. The storm makes him restless. It makes him want to throw off the blankets and run.

He sits up suddenly. Sheets flap into the air and fly away like ghosts, leaving him sitting bollock-naked on the bed. Specks of rain tantalise his skin and send shivers up his back-bone. It takes a little while for the vibrations and shockwaves to quit. Once he has adjusted to the sharp air, his body feels electric and fresh.

He eases himself gently off the bed and steps down into the rustling grass. He runs, swishing through the wetness. He feels stronger and more alive with each step. Sucking in a deep breath, he leaps the back wall. The coldness feels like icewater gushing down his throat. He lands with a plop, then splatters through the long grass to the bank. Beyond the bumpy back wall, fields of bracken swing in the breeze, rolling up to the high-standing rocks which sparkle in the moonlight like a movie star's teeth. There is a swamp ahead. It glitters moonbeams at him as he approaches. He leaps that too. For a terrible hanging second he thinks that he is going to splash in amongst the tadpoles and feel the shock of cold water enveloping him. But he plonks down on the far side and keeps running. Now he knows he can do anything. At the rocks, wind lifts him from behind and lightning goes off around him like flashbulbs. He flits upwards like a kite. From the topmost rock, he sees the entire hill humming and flickering and sparkling beneath him like a toy fair.

After pausing for a moment, he turns his back on home and tears down the other side of the rocks into the dark fields towards the cliffs. As he runs, he yodels just for the hell of it. 'Ow-oo-ow-oo-ah,' he yells, cupping his hands to his mouth just as he did when he was a kid. Every dog on the hill howls back. Then the cats start up, mewling as though in agony. The noise wakes up the babies in their cribs and gets them wailing too. Soon lights come on in all the houses and doors slam open and the air cackles and snorts and belches with people yelling at their animals to shut the fuck up for Jaysus' sake.

Everyone was shocked when Parnell went for the postman. Before that, Parnell had been the meekest dog on the hill. People said he was the type who wouldn't even attack his dinner.

'That dog's sick,' the postman shouted from the bottom of the drive as Frankie and Ray held on to the barking, snarling family pet. 'From now on, yis can collect yer letters at the post office.'

The morning after, Parnell attacked Mr Figgis from next door. Then he bit the breadman. Within a week, he was the most notorious dog on the hill. Even Alsatians avoided him.

'The dog's gone mental,' Frankie said. 'We have to do something.'

'He's just overexcited,' Ma said. 'Give him a fig roll and he'll be grand.'

For two weeks they received no mail, no deliveries, no visitors except for Nelson, whom even Parnell was reluctant to cross.

'I can't understand it,' Frankie told Nelson. 'Up until now, Parnell was the only dog I ever met who was afraid of cats.'

'Maybe he was abused when he was a pup and it's only coming out now.'

'Yeah, sure...'

'Well, you never know.'

When Mrs Figgis and some of the neighbours called with a petition asking for Parnell to be muzzled or put down, Ma told them to go about their own business. 'Nobody touches our family dog,' she shouted after them. 'Get off my property or I'll bite you myself.'

Immediately afterwards, Ma beckoned Frankie and put him in charge of Parnell. 'Don't let him start with anyone who isn't family,' she warned.

Parnell wagged his tail and licked Frankie's hand and face. He even let Hopper come to visit without barking at him. Every time the dog got excited, Frankie threw him a fig roll. When Parnell had eaten an entire packet, Nelson bent down for a look.

'He seems all right now. Maybe he had a toothache or something.'

To take his mind off Ma and Parnell and his dreadful job bulb-picking which left him too tired to speak most evenings, and to overcome his sense of foreboding about the exam results and his fear of not getting into college and all the rest of the things that were bothering him, Frankie came up with the idea of converting the garage in to a rehearsal studio for rock bands.

The garage was full of rubbish and old furniture and dust. It had been years since Da had parked the car there. All he had to do was clear out the debris, soundproof the walls with eggboxes and hire somebody to fix up the wiring. After that, he could rent it out to every punk band in the city. Soon, bands would be screaming to get in. He'd make stacks. He would be able to give up bulb-picking. He wouldn't have to worry about the exam results or about getting into college. He could buy a leather jacket with studs on it. First, though, he'd have to ask Ma.

Ma was in the kitchen sitting on the high stool when Frankie found her. She was smoking a cigarette and listening to a Gaelic football match on the radio. 'Mayo are winning by two points,' she said.

She gazed out of the window as Frankie told her what he wanted to do. He half expected her to yell at him, but instead she told him dreamily: 'Go ahead... but make sure you get a good electrician to wire it up properly. And keep an eye on that bloody dog.'

Nelson and Hopper refused to have anything to do with Frankie's plan. As far as they were concerned, he was crazy.

'Sounds like a lot of hard work to me,' Hopper said.

'Think about all the punk bands.'

'I hate punk rock,' Nelson said. 'I wouldn't piss on Johnny Rotten if he was on fire.'

'OK, but don't come crying to me when I'm driving around in my Rolls,' Frankie said and walked off in a huff.

'You'll have to learn to drive first,' Nelson said darkly, and he and Hopper sniggered through their noses.

Davy Dudley was six foot two with a wide, square face and small blue eyes that blinked a lot. Most people thought he looked like a horse. At tennis club dances, he was always asking girls if they wanted to go outside for a bit of 'nicky-hooky'. The girls always turned him down. Recently, Davy had spiked his hair and stuck rows of safety pins along the lapels of his green velvet jacket. Everyone said he still looked like a horse.

Davy was all on for the rehearsal studio. He was mad keen on Frankie's sister, Maggie, so they did a deal: Davy would wire up the garage, and Frankie would help fix Davy up with Maggie.

'I'm an electrical wizard,' he bragged. 'My instructors at Tech said they'd never seen anything like me in their lives.'

They started work on Saturday morning. For hours they carried out broken chairs and tables and bits of wood, mangy old carpets and mangled lawnmowers, rusty toasters and wrecked radios and crumpled cardboard boxes, bricks and brush-handles and bedposts, every one of which unearthed millions of tiny crawling things. They piled the rubbish in a heap on the bank at the side of the driveway.

'Where's Maggie?' Davy asked, grinning, whenever they took a break.

'She's around—you'll see her later.'

Davy's blue eyes sparkled. 'We could form a band. I'm a brilliant guitarist. At the last place I lived, people used to say I was a young Clapton. You can be singer, Nelson can play bass and Hopper can go on drums. Whatya think?'

'Yeah, maybe...'

'The chicks will go mental for us. Nick-nick-nickyhooky, what?'

'OK, OK, just quit saying "nicky-hooky", it's driving me insane.'

Later, Nelson and Hopper arrived. They had decided that helping out with the garage was a lot better than hanging around the cliff beach eyeing up girls who were too snobby to talk to anyone. Maggie wandered in. She stood in the doorway and looked around sneeringly at the pockmarked wall, the dusty floor and at Davy and Nelson and Hopper who were lugging out a broken-down sofa. Awestruck, Davy let his end of the sofa drop and Nelson called him a stupid fucking gronk.

Frankie stood in front of his sister. 'What do you want?'

'Nuthin,' Maggie shrugged, and drifted out again.

When she had gone, Davy came up to Frankie. 'Put in a good word for us, will you? I sense a chemistry between us.'

When all the rubbish had been removed, Ma came out with a plate of hot sausages. 'Very good,' she said looking around at the bare dusty walls. 'It's a pity my son doesn't work this hard around the house.'

After tea, Parnell slipped out of the house and hid on the bank of the driveway with Noelie. Noelie threw rocks at passing cars and Parnell barked at everyone who walked by. For a while, they had great fun. The fun stopped when someone called the police. Ma had to do a lot of fancy talking to persuade the police to let Parnell off.

'OK,' the young country cop warned, 'but if this ever happens again, I'll have to take the dog away.'

Ma stood in the doorway with her hands on her hips and watched the squad car drive off.

'You'd think the police in this country would have better things to do than be going around persecuting defenceless family pets.'

Dawn wanted to know why Parnell was being so bold. Ma sighed and sat Dawn down on the big black armchair in the study. She thought for a moment, then she called everyone in to hear what was wrong with the dog.

'Parnell is descended from Bran and Sceolín, the famous hunting dogs of Finn McCool and the warriors of the Fianna. Those dogs could run faster than a deer and were stronger than twenty men. They were noble animals and the warriors treated them like friends. They all ate the same food and slept on the same blankets. Long ago, Niamh of the Golden Hair led Oisín and Finn, the warriors of the Fianna, and their hounds Bran and Sceolín across the secret path of moonlight on the sea to live forever in Tír na nÓg—the Land of Eternal Youth. That's where all Celtic warriors go to when they decide to leave this world. So you see, it's not easy for a dog like Parnell to put up with stupid postmen and ignorant policemen and that fool of a West Brit Figgis next door. From now on, I want you all to treat Parnell with care.'

After that, Ma told Frankie to keep Parnell with him at all times; whenever he was working on the garage he could keep the dog tied to the door. Ray was told to take Noelie for plenty of long walks.

The following morning, Davy ran a lead from the plug in Frankie's room. He had to chisel a deep groove in the window-frame to get the window closed, but Frankie didn't mind; as soon as the rehearsal studio was in operation and making money, he would buy a new window, maybe build himself a new room. There was no end to what he might do.

Ray went over to the window and flicked a wood shaving off the sill.

'I don't think Ma's going to be very pleased,' he said.

'Don't fucken tell her then.'

'Tell her what? I haven't seen anything,' Ray said and strolled off, whistling.

Soon Davy had rigged up a lightbulb, a heater, an old radio and a set of revolving red and orange disco lights stolen from the tennis club. Then he got out his hacksaw and began sawing the speaker section of Frankie's portable record player in half.

'Hey, hang on a minute,' Frankie said, shaken out of his daydreaming.

'Trust me, will ye?'

Something about the baretoothed zeal with which Davy drove the hacksaw made Frankie hesitate. By the time he got over it, Davy was cheerfully hanging the severed parts on the wall as far apart as the wires would stretch.

'See,' Davy announced with a flourish, 'now it's perfect stereo.'

That night, Davy stopped Maggie in the driveway and asked her out. For a moment, Maggie was stunned.

'Don't be stew-pit. I already have a boyfriend,' she said.

'That's OK, I don't mind sharing.'

'No way.'

'Aw go on,' Davy implored as Maggie walked up the drive. 'You won't know for sure till you've tried. I'll borrow me Pa's Jag. We'll have a rapid time.'

Maggie told Davy to fuck off.

'Aaah, I know you don't mean it,' Davy said.

They worked on the garage each night after work for a week. By noon on the following Saturday, everything was ready. An old mattress and cushions had been arranged on the floor. In the corner was a beaten-up sofa and a couple of rickety wooden chairs. Eggboxes had been nailed over the two windows. Frankie's record player and records rested on a small bedside table Nelson had found in a skip. Everyone thought it looked great.

Davy made doubly sure that the lights, record player, radio, heater and fan were connected to the main light-switch. 'A flick of a finger and it will be like walking into heaven,' he boasted. 'It just needs a Sex Pistols poster.'

With great solemnity, Nelson removed Elvis's Golden Records Vol 3 from its sleeve and placed it on the record deck. He cued the needle at the start of 'Marie's the Name (of his Latest Flame)'—his favourite Elvis song of the moment. 'Gotta have a song from the King,' he said, 'otherwise, it's not really official.' Frankie decided that Davy should have the honour of flicking the switch. Davy was, after all, the electrical wizard who had fixed the place up. Davy gave a silly grin. 'After this, your sister will definitely go out with me.'

Davy flicked the switch.

There was a bang and a bright blue flash, followed by a distant 'ka-boom' from the house. The needle skated across

Elvis, making a low shriek like a cat falling down an empty well. The lightbulb popped from its socket and exploded on the floor, causing everyone to duck. There was a sharp crackling noise—and then silence.

'Mother of Moses,' Nelson said.

A few seconds later, there was a yell from the kitchen.

Through a gap in the eggboxes in the side window, they saw Ma yanking open the back door and marching out with a mighty stern face on her. She had a frying pan in her hand.

'Me tea's ready,' Davy said and ran.

'Mine too,' Hopper said and followed.

'G'luck,' Nelson said.

Frankie stood like a dummy until Ma came round the corner and then he too took off.

'Blackguards!' Ma screamed and flung the frying pan after them.

Ma had to hire a master electrician to get the electrics in the house working again. The master electrician said that only a maniac could have made such a balls of things. It was pure luck that nobody had been fried. Frankie returned at teatime and kept very quiet. It was two days before Ma talked to him and then it was only to inform him that Davy Dudley was barred from the house for life.

'If that fool ever shows his big horse's face around here again, I'll have him cremated on the spot,' Ma said.

* * *

Ma was invited to Limerick for a big Fianna Fáil meeting. Her country needed her, she declared grandly. It was people like her who gave the party leadership its direction and common sense. She went into town with Maggie in a taxi and came back wearing a bright pink floral dress-suit, black high heels and a long black shawl which trailed along the ground after her.

Before she left, she called everyone into the kitchen. 'I'll be gone for a night,' she announced, 'but I know I can trust my family to behave themselves while I'm gone.'

Then she took each of them aside in secret and made them swear to inform on the others if there was any hanky-panky. Everyone promised that they would.

The moment Ma's taxi was out of sight, Frankie dashed to the phone. 'I've got a Free House tonight,' he told Nelson, 'meet me at the Summit.'

The party started after the Summit pub closed. Teenagers came from all over the hill. Everyone brought sixpacks or bottles of wine. Somebody brought a barrel of Smithwicks that they'd 'found' in the yard behind the Summit pub. Cyril McLean showed up with an ounce of Lebanese Red. By midnight, the house was jammed. For a while, Frankie tried to confine the action to the kitchen, study and dining-room. He gave up when he found Bobby Gallo and Jennie Brady wriggling like fish at the bottom of Ma's wardrobe.

Maggie and Pierre Colcannon retired to her room early on and locked the door. Davy Dudley wandered around with a droopy face on him like an old bloodhound. Later, he drank a half-bottle of sherry and passed out in the bath. Frankie kept hoping that Romy Casey would appear. After a while, though, he heard that Romy and her friend Jayne Wayne had gone down the country for the weekend. Typical, he figured. Noelie went around clunking kissing couples on the head with his can of beans and saying 'hello'. Ray had to bring him into their parents' bedroom and read stories to him until he fell asleep.

When all the beer was gone, Frankie put 'The Boys Are Back in Town' on the record player and he and Hopper and Nelson and Cyril McLean jumped on top of the living-room table. They clutched brooms as guitars and yelled the words and made faces and mimed powerchords and bass runs and crashing drums and dropped to their knees for the guitar riffs. Mo and Jo and the other hippies from the town danced about in front of the makeshift stage as though at a real rock concert. Dawn stood in the doorway cuddling her dolly, watching with big eyes. Afterwards Frankie tried to get off with Mo, but she told him she never went out with a friend's relatives. Frankie said that was OK, he was only kidding anyhow.

During a lull, Hopper hung the speakers out the front-room windows and put on 'Beat on the Brat' by The Ramones at full volume. All the boys in the house sang along:

'Beat on the Brat, Beat on the Brat, Beat on the Brat
with a Baseball Bat, Oh Yeah, Oh Yeah, Oh-oh Yeah...'

Lights went on all over the hill. People came to complain, but Parnell chased them off.

At first light, when everyone else had gone home, Nelson got out Dawn's tricycle, Hopper mounted Ray's old wooden go-kart and Frankie squeezed into Noelie's bumper car. They sailed down the driveway, skidded around the corner and rattled down the hill towards the town. Cyril McLean clattered after them on the back of a rusty Quinnsworth trolley, whooping like an Apache. There was no traffic at that time of the morning so they had a race to see who would be first to the harbour. They performed what they thought were daredevil stunts and tried every trick they could to make one another crash into the kerb. Their screams and curses woke up most people in the road. Whizzing down was a lot of fun, but trudging back up the hill hauling transport, which had inexplicably turned heavy and cumbersome, was exhausting.

When Frankie got back, drained and puffing from the steep climb, Davy Dudley was on the roof, having tied himself to the chimney with a length of rope. He wanted to talk to Maggie, he said; he was going to stay on the roof until Maggie agreed to go out with him. Frankie was too tired and hung over and depressed to know what to do about the situation. Things were sort of out of control now, he felt: whatever was going to happen would happen anyway. If Davy Dudley had decided to tie himself to the roof because he was mental about Maggie then that was nothing to do with him. All he could do now was to go inside, gather the empty bottles and cigarette butts, and tidy away the party debris. So that's what he did.

Ma came home to find a bunch of people in the driveway exchanging bets on whether Davy Dudley would last the night. She stood and glared at them until they shuffled away. Then she ordered Davy to get down out of that. Davy gave her a pained ironical smile and explained that nobody can stand in the way of love.

'Love is bigger than any of us,' he said.

'Right,' Ma said and went inside. She came back out with a ladder, climbed up onto the roof and went after Davy with a mop. Davy slid down the drainpipe, hit the ground and ran. Ma stood on the roof with the mop by her side like a spear, her black shawl flowing behind her in the wind, and watched him go.

'I can't leave this bloody place for a minute,' she said.

Next morning, Parnell nipped Mr Figgis on the leg as he walked past the driveway.

'OK, that's it,' Mr Figgis said.

At lunchtime two policemen arrived to take Parnell away. The dog was dangerous, they said. They'd given fair warning last time.

'Ye're a disgrace to your country,' Ma told them, then stormed inside to phone the Minister for Justice.

Maggie and Ray and Dawn watched silently from the porch as the policeman made Frankie bring Parnell down to the squad car. Parnell's eyes were wide and his tail was between his legs. Frankie lifted the dog into a booth and turned away. One of the policemen closed the hatch and locked it. As the squad car drove off, Dawn cried.

That evening, Ma took Dawn on her knee and explained that Parnell was now in Tír na nÓg, far across the water with Finn McCool and Oisín and all the great Celtic warriors, and Finn's famous hounds, Bran and Sceolín. Now Parnell would never get old and would always be happy, she said.

Dawn considered for a moment. 'Are there any fig rolls in Tír na nÓg?' she sniffled.

First thing next morning, Ma and Dawn went up to the Summit shop and bought a packet of fig rolls, two sheets of cardboard, a roll of coloured paper and lots of string. They made a brightly coloured box, put the packet of fig rolls in it and posted it to: 'Parnell Griffin, Tír na nÓg, Section for Very Special Dogs'.

10

THE FREEDOM FIGHTER

It was a bright morning. The sun sizzled in the sky like a great fried egg. Ray reckoned it was so hot that even the flies were too pooped to move. After breakfast, Ma rose to her feet and hushed everyone. She had good news, she announced: one of Ireland's greatest patriots was coming to tea. This Freedom Fighter was going to reunite North and South and kick the Brits back into the sea. He was also going to give Ma's local Fianna Fáil party committee a few tips on how to oust the local Fine Gael TD, whom Ma called a 'pig-ignorant blueshirt bastard who wasn't fit to suck cowshite through a straw'.

'I want an honour guard of Griffin children on the porch to greet him. We'll show him this family at its best.'

'Aw, Ma, I'm supposed to meet Nelson,' Frankie said.

'Too bad, mister. You can just invest a little time in your family for once.'

First the honour guard was sent up to the shops to get rashers and sausages, a dozen six-packs of Guinness and forty Carrolls. Later, Frankie went up again to fetch a bottle of whiskey. Seventeen years old and still doing messages, he thought to himself, what a pain.

Throughout the morning and afternoon, they stood on the porch and kept watch in case the visitor decided to show up early. You never could tell with these freedom fighters, Ma warned; they didn't keep the same hours as normal people. Frankie tried to slip away by ambling towards the back of the house as if going for a stroll, but Maggie was wise to his tricks. She yelled that she'd tell Ma on him and then Ma would confiscate the dollars Da was sending him from New York for helping out around the house.

'All right, keep your voice down, will ye?'

For a while, Frankie mooched around the front. Next he tried kicking the ball around the garden. But he got sick of chasing it down the hill every time it went through a gap in the hedge. So he went back to mooching around and feeling sorry for himself. All his schemes had failed, he thought to himself gloomily; the Dalek was in bits, the garage had been a disaster and his summer work as a bulb-picker was slowly turning him into a zombie. It was a good thing the bulb-picking was being cut back to just mornings next week otherwise he felt sure that, sooner or later, he would have slumped over dead on a mucky furrow. Then they would all have been very sorry and it would have been too late. The image of Ma and Da's pained faces at his funeral made him give a wry smile.

Last week he had felt so desperate that he had gone down to the harbour to ask for a berth on Nelson's fishing boat, but the captain had refused to take him. Afterwards, Nelson had told him it was because he was too tall and at sea tall blokes were notorious for always getting knocked overboard. Skippers didn't have time to be turning the boat around every ten minutes just to pick people out of the drink, Nelson had explained. 'But you're tall,' Frankie had objected. 'That's different,' Nelson had shrugged nonchalantly, 'I'm good.'

Now Frankie felt that he had no one in the world to turn to for advice about his situation. Nelson and Hopper were bored with his problems by now, talking to Davy Dudley was like talking to a fencepost, and of course Da was away just as he had been throughout most of Frankie's life.

He had never really talked much to Da about things anyway, but all the same he felt insecure when his father was not around. There was a huge presence missing from the house as well as a sense of something important having been tampered with, as though someone had replaced the sturdy tiled roof with a flimsy paper replica that was certain to burst apart at any second to let in rain and floods and hailstones and God knows what else. Only the sight of Da's car coming up the drive could make things right. For an instant, Frankie experienced again the delicious anticipation he had felt as a kid lying in bed on nights before Da came home, listening for the roar of the car and the sudden sweep of headlights across the wall of the back yard, thinking about the presents his father was bringing back for him.

If the freedom fighter didn't turn up soon, Frankie was going to miss the meeting at the Summit to arrange the big barbecue on the cliff beach. He and Nelson and Hopper were planning a massive bonfire with loads of booze and joints as long as your arm; every fine thing on the hill would be invited; Davy Dudley was going to rig up a sound system that he said would be heard in Wales; and Hopper had promised to steal a whole pig from his uncle's butcher's shop which they would roast on a spit. It was going to be really something, the best barbecue ever seen on the hill.

And black-eyed, long-legged Romy Casey would be there, too. The word was that Romy had finally broken it off with Bobby Gallo. About time, Frankie thought; he hated Bobby's leather jacket and his Frank Zappa albums and his big shiny Kawasaki. Especially the big shiny Kawasaki. He also hated the fact that Bobby had been going out with Romy since the beginning of last summer. It really pissed him off when Bobby did wheelies on people's front lawns with Romy on the back. Maybe Romy had finally got fed up being dumped into flowerbeds.

For his part, Frankie was going to borrow Da's silent movie projector to show Keystone Kops and Charlie Chaplin films on the cliff walls. It would be like having his own open-air cinema. He was sure it was going to be a wonderful night.

He decided to reason with Maggie one last time. Approaching her, he kept his voice low and conspiratorial so that Ray and Dawn wouldn't hear.

'Listen, cover for us, will ye? Then you and your pals can come to the secret barbecue we're arranging on the cliff beach this Saturday.'

'Hmmmmph,' Maggie said and stared off into the distance.

She was always snubbing him like that. It drove him mad.

'Go on, will ye? It'll be great. You can bring Pierre if you want to.'

'Pierre wouldn't go to your crappy party.'

'Hey, what about me?' Ray chipped in from the doorway. 'I'll go.'

'You're too young.'

'I am not.'

'OK, then you're too thick.' Ray narrowed his eyes and did his John Wayne face.

'Them's fightin' words, pardner,' he drawled. 'Say it again and you'll be going on a one-way trip to Boot Hill.'

'Shut your face.'

'I wanna go too,' Dawn cried.

'Christ, now see what you've started.'

Maggie shrugged her golden curls. 'It's your problem. I don't want to go to any crummy *barby-cue* anyway. If you're having it, it's bound to be crap.'

Frankie lost his temper. 'Fucken barge.'

'Frankie-wankey,' Maggie replied sweetly.

'Barge.'

'Wankey.'

'What's going on out there?'

'Nothing, Ma.'

'Ain't nuthin' Ah can't handle, lady,' John Wayne said.

For the rest of the afternoon, there was silence on the porch. The sun blazed down and made them hot and irritable. Ma conked out in the easy chair in the kitchen. Occasionally, they heard her low snoring. It broke the monotony of the squealing and buzzing and grinding of the rich kids' cars as they charged up and down the hill.

'Still no sign?' Maggie asked.

'Maybe he's been shot,' Ray cracked.

'Don't be stew-pit. People only get shot up north.'

'Well, he could have been kidnapped.'

At the first dong of the six o'clock church bells from the town, a man trundled into the driveway. He was short and fat with dark hair which was plastered like ink across his scalp, and had a big red face that was awash in streams of sweat. He wheezed like an old dog as he waddled up the slope. Frankie was sure the man was about to have a heart attack right there on the tarmac.

As soon as he saw Frankie and Dawn and Ray watching him from the porch, the visitor managed a jagged smile.

'What about yis?' he croaked.

Then he sat down heavily on the grass bank. Dawn dropped her dolly on the porch and scooted into the house, dress flying. 'Mammy, Mammy, the Freedom Fighter's here.'

The freedom fighter's name was Billy Sheridan and he was pleased to meet everyone. He didn't come across as someone who was going to kick the Brits back into the sea. Instead, he looked relieved to have made it up the steps alive. Ma showed him into the study, took his coat, fluttered about like an ecstatic nun and delivered many flowing benedictions in Irish before sitting him down in Da's favourite black leather armchair.

'Jest call me Bully,' Billy winked and slapped Frankie on the back. 'Lordy, that sun is a killer. For a while there, Ah tot Ah wus in da Sahara.'

He sat back in the huge black armchair with his feet swinging at least three inches off the carpet. He smiled at everyone as Ma poured him a glass of foaming Guinness. Frankie thought he looked like a garden gnome.

'Ah shouldn't really, Ah'm sapposed ta be takin' it easy—hehehe,' he squeaked.

Then he drained the glass in one gulp. Ma immediately poured him another.

'Sure it's good for you. You need the strength after that dreadful walk,' Ma said.

Ma said it was disgraceful that he had had to walk up the hill on a sunny day like today; it was obvious that every bus crew on the northside was off snoozing or boozing in the pub or gallivanting on the beach with floozies.

'I blame the Brits. They banjaxed our transport service with their imperialism and their genocide and their hoity-toity ways. Anyone can see that.'

'Aye, anyone can see that.'

Ma and Billy discussed British government policy in Ireland over the past eight hundred years. Ma said that the British had sabotaged the entire Irish nation and almost destroyed the people's language, culture and religion. In her opinion the Brits had treated the Irish in exactly the same way as Hitler had treated the Jews. Now that she thought about it, wasn't it a great pity that old Hitler hadn't bombed the Brits back to the Stone Age during the Blitz.

'Aah, but there's no justice in the world,' she lamented, raising her hands imploringly to heaven.

'Aye, no justice,' the freedom fighter agreed.

'You know the Brits have a secret listening post in Dublin Castle. They've been tapping our phone for years. I can hear the bastard breathing on the other end every time I pick up the receiver.'

'Is thot a fact?' Billy asked.

'Of course,' Ma said in astonishment. 'Sure the phones in this country haven't worked properly since the Brits blew up the GPO in 1916. Everyone knows that.'

There was silence for a moment as everyone digested Ma's pronouncements. Then Billy creaked on the armchair and looked grave. He studied the froth at the bottom of his glass.

'Er, ye wouldn't have another one a these lying about, would ye missus G.?'

An hour later, Frankie finally escaped from the house and joined up with Nelson and Hopper at the Summit to plan the big barbecue. Later they ambushed the lighthouse-keeper's son at the Hill roundabout. 'Ah no, not again,' little Cyril McLean whinged as Nelson and Hopper took his arms and escorted him up the road to the Summit car park. 'I wish you fuckers would leave me alone.'

They plonked him on the wall and squished in either side of him so he couldn't make a break for it.

'We just want a few words,' Frankie said pleasantly, 'we're really doing you a favour.'

Cyril sat with his skinny shoulders slumped forward and his pinched little nose pointed at his shoes. Any second now he knew one of them would put dog turds in his pockets or drop a Tayto Crisp bag filled with water on his head. Then they'd all have a big laugh. Oh yeah. Big joke. Last time, that big swine Nelson had set fire to his tie. Cyril couldn't understand why they picked on him. He guessed they were jealous of his blazers.

Everyone regarded Cyril as a pain in the hole. He showed up where he wasn't wanted and gossiped and told tales like an old fishwife. Even adults avoided him. Nelson said the only thing Cyril McLean was good for was target practice. Whenever they were really stuck for something to do, Frankie and Nelson and Hopper waylaid Cyril and committed atrocities on him. Apart from that, nobody wanted anything to do with him.

Now and again, though, Cyril did manage to get hold of some excellent dope. Whenever that happened he became extremely popular, mainly because nobody else on the hill— not even Stony Rogers the King of the Hill Weirdos whom everyone hated because of his uncanny resemblance to Charles Manson—could roll a nine-skin joint the way Cyril could. Once the dope was gone, though, Cyril became target practice again.

It had taken Frankie nearly an hour to convince Nelson and Hopper that Cyril was essential to the barbecue.

'He's a gronk,' Nelson had protested. 'Nelson Fitzgerald does not hang around with gronks.'

But when Frankie had explained his great idea for turning a simple beach barbecue into the Party of the Century, Nelson had grudgingly agreed to go along.

'But if the little fart starts whingeing, I'll burst him—I'm giving you fair warning.'

Now, Frankie stood in front of Cyril and put his hands on his hips. He told Cyril they were throwing the biggest and best beach barbecue ever seen on the hill. They needed his help. Without it, there would be no party. If Cyril agreed to help out, he would be doing himself a good turn. He would become their new partner.

Cyril smiled. This was more like it. They had finally accepted him. He always knew it would happen someday.

'All you have to do is slip us into the lighthouse on Saturday night so that we can take over the beam. We just want to show a few old Charlie Chaplin movies on the cliff face. Your Da will never know.'

The smile fell off Cyril's face. His eyes turned glassy and his lip curved in a slow curl of resignation. He should have guessed. This was even worse than a dog turd in the pocket. It would also be a lot harder to explain.

'My Pop will kick me out.'

His pinched face begged Frankie to tell him it was all a gag.

'Aw, for fuck's sake,' Nelson said.

'Don't be such a spare,' Hopper said.

Frankie laughed. 'The lighthouse is fully automatic. Your pop will sleep through the whole thing. We'll be in and out of there in an hour, I promise.'

Cyril stubbed his toes into the dust a few times while he thought it over. 'What if a ship hits the rocks and sinks? I don't want to be responsible for that. I'm not that kind of person.'

'Ships have radar these days. They don't really need light-houses any more.'

Cyril still looked doubtful.

'Besides, we'll only take over if it's a clear night.'

'Look,' Nelson said, 'if a mist comes in, we'll honk the horn a few times. Then all the ships will fuck off with them-selves. Happy now?'

Cyril stood up and put his hands in the pockets of his trousers. He kicked a pebble. He sulked. Frankie offered him a cigarette. 'Don't want one,' Cyril said in a tiny voice.

Hopper grinned in an attempt to make Cyril feel more at ease. 'We can tie you up. Then it will look like the work of professional lighthouse hijackers.'

'No way, then I'd miss the party.'

'Oh yeah, never thought of that.'

Nelson ran out of patience. 'It's very simple: help us or I'll give you a box in the gob.'

That was what Cyril had been dreading. He took off like a missile down the hill towards home.

Nelson ran after him, but Frankie called him back. 'Let him go—skinny little fucks like him always chicken out.'

'Next time I get him, I'm going to sit on his face and fart till he goes purple.'

'We'll have a barbecue without him or his Da's crappy lighthouse. Who needs him?'

But Nelson wanted revenge. He took a black marker out of his pocket, checked to make sure there was nobody at the pub's outside tables, then went across to the whitewashed wall of the Summit car park where he wrote: 'Cyril McLean has a small tool' in large thick black letters.

'They'll never get that off. His family will see it and his children and his children's children. It'll be his epitaph.'

That night, Ma threw a party in Billy's honour. She invited all her friends from the hill as well as a bunch of people from the local Fianna Fáil party. Everyone brought a bottle of whiskey and a six-pack. Ma sent up to the Summit pub for cooked chickens and buttered bread rolls. When Frankie got home, all the lights in the house were on and the doors and windows were open. Noelie was dancing naked in the front garden. 'Hello, Frak,' Noelie said as he handed Frankie a can of beans with the wrapper torn off.

Inside, every room reverberated with loud laughter and arguments and bouts of shouting mixed with speechmaking. Somewhere in the back, a deep male voice boomed, 'Glory-O, Glory-O / To the Bold Fenian Men'. In the study, Ma played ballad records on the old, red, wooden gramophone and led people in a singalong. Eyes glittering and long dark hair flowing behind like a flag, Ma looked young and beautiful and carefree and wild. She clapped her hands in the air when the chorus came around. 'C'mon, the lot of ye, sing out now:

'Every man must stand behind
The Men Behind the Wire...'

In the corner, the freedom fighter was perched on the arm of the old black armchair, telling a dozen spellbound listeners about the time he was attacked by a British tank during the Battle of the Bogside. 'It jest came round the corner and started shootin'at me. There wur young fellas fallin' all over the place, heads shot off. So Ah took up a petrol bomb and hooshed it at thum. It musta hit the ammunition or something cos' Ah swear to God the tank jest blew all to bits so it did. War's a terrble buzzness, so it is, a terrble buzzness, but it wuz thum or me...Ah'm jest an ordinary workin' man doin' ma duty...Eh, tell us, pal, anytin' left in that wee bottle there?'

Somebody grabbed a bottle and poured him another drink. 'Ah tell yis, mabbe yis should lob a few wee petrol bombs at yer mon the Fine Gaeler way yonder up the hill—yis mightn't win the election but it'd sure liven it up so it would.'

Everyone roared with laughter. 'Good man, yerself,' someone shouted. The freedom fighter looked up and saw Frankie. He smiled and raised his glass. 'What about ye?' he said. Without waiting for a reply, he turned back to his audience. 'D'ye know what this wee town needs? A gude riot, that's what. It'd be the makings of yis, so it would...'

In the kitchen, Mr Vincent was on top of the washing machine, delivering a passionate speech warning against the evils of Russian Communism. 'All I want to know is, does the man in the street get the same wage as the top guy in the Kremlin?' he bellowed.

'Yes,' Ray shouted. 'Two quid a week and all the vodka he can drink.'

Everyone laughed and Mr Vincent's face went red.

'Ye wouldn't be that smart with me if yer mother was in here, would ye?' Mr Vincent snarled.

'If my mother was in here, you wouldn't be on top of our washing machine,' Ray answered.

The crowd roared again. Ray took a bow to whoops and whistles and loud applause. Agitated and waving his arms for quiet, Mr Vincent succeeded only in putting his foot through the lid of the washing machine, where it got stuck—to hoots and squeals and slow handclapping.

After a while, someone helped him get free.

Frankie moved around and poached a few bottles of beer. He stayed well away from Ma in case she tried to get him to sing a ballad or recite poetry for her guests. Later he wandered into the hallway where the freedom fighter was taking up a collection on behalf of himself. People filed by and reverently handed him folded tens and twenties. 'Ah, thank ye, thank ye, ye're very kind, God bless ye,' he said and put the bills into his inside pocket.

At first light, Ma went off to bed. Soon afterwards, the guests began stumbling home. Mrs Donovan stepped off the porch and fell into the front garden. She lay there roaring her head off with her legs in the air until Maggie helped her up and guided her down the steps. Frankie and Ray stood with flashlights and directed the others to the driveway.

In a little while, only Mr Vincent was left. 'I do not require any help from anybody,' he said proudly and wobbled off. 'Ignatius Vincent has never leaned on anybody and never will.'

He skidded down the steps, tumbled into the bushes but righted himself with a display of haughty indignation, then staggered all the way to the end of the driveway where Noelie got him right between the eyes with a can of beans.

Frankie and Ray and Maggie were in the kitchen finishing off the whiskey when Dawn came in all sleepy-eyed to tell them that the freedom fighter was asleep in the toilet bowl. They went to see and found him sprawled over the bowl, hands in the water and trousers wrapped around his face.

'Why does the freedom fighter have his head in his pants?' Dawn asked.

'Because he just does, that's why,' Frankie said.

'It's just adult stuff,' Ray said consolingly. 'You wouldn't understand.'

It took them half an hour to drag the unconscious guest to the living-room and put him on the sofa with a blanket over him.

In the morning, the freedom fighter rose early and said that he was very sorry but he couldn't stay for breakfast. 'Ah've important buzzness up in the wee North,' he announced mysteriously. 'Yis know what Ah mean.'

Then he borrowed twenty quid from Ma and took a taxi down the hill to the bus terminus. Everyone lined the porch to wave goodbye.

'Now, children,' Ma said. 'Count yourselves lucky. There goes a man ye'll remember for the rest of your lives.'

11
HOPPER

He watched the bright yellow flames whooshing up into the darkness. This one would burn for a week. In a little while, he knew, they would take over the lighthouse and fix the beam on the cliff face to show Charlie Chaplin movies. Nobody would ever forget that. He stepped off the edge of the cliff and glided down to land on the beach. In the centre of the bonfire, a pig was being roasted on a spit. The Hill Gang and Summit Girls sat in a circle passing around joints and laughing and nodding to the thump of loud rock and roll. Nelson knelt at the far side, sipping a bottle of Harp, holding hands with Patty Gargan. Beside them Cyril McLean moaned and Hopper shrugged and got up to turn the pig, Jayne Wayne and Romy Casey looked cool and dark and mysterious next to pinch-faced Bobby Gallo who sweated in a heavy leather jacket which he was too vain to take off. Raggedy-haired Stony Rogers, the King of the Hill Weirdos, squatted on a dune blowing dope clouds out of a grass pipe while all around him his hairy hippy followers stretched out their hands for a blast. A couple of yards away

Maggie wrapped herself around Pierre Colcannon as Mo and Jo and their fellas clumped together murmuring like druids at a sacrifice, dolloping out lashings of blood-red wine into paper cups. Gap-toothed Vinnie Cassidy and blimp-bellied Jack the Rack and their mates sneered at everything as they slugged Guinness and eyed up the fine things who were clustered together at the side, out of the wind and smoke, trying to start up a bit of a dance. At the far edge of the blaze, horsefaced Davy Dudley stood tall as a telephone pole on top of a massive trembling speaker, with his back to the lot of them. He was pissing a long bright golden stream out into the sand and, with his head back, was roaring 'I'm Down On the Bee-ches. Looking at the Pee-ches' by The Stranglers which was blasting out from underneath him like doomsday.

Romy Casey stood up from the sparkily exploding fire and smiled at Frankie. Surprised, he smiled back. She arched her back and stretched and raised up her hands to spread long elegant fingers at the starry black sky until something cricked. Then she straightened up and padded with soft dainty clips across the churned-up sand to where he was. 'Hi,' she said, 'you made it then.' 'Yeah, I did,' he said. She looked so cute standing there tall and slender, her lovely round face with its little snub nose and thin lips and big dark eyes framed by a short pageboy. 'Would you like to go for a walk?' he heard himself saying. Romy nodded her head. 'Yeah, sure, why not?' she said. He could scarcely believe it. His little heart did a yo-yo into the pit of his stomach and up again. They slushed off along the dunes to the rocks at the far end of the beach where water whished and sprayed tiny flecks of wet onto their skin. After a minute, she slipped her delicate hand into his.

Then he was holding her. Her breath smelled like pine needles mixed with Guinness. She kissed him with the passion of a lusty vampirella in some old starchy horror flick and he kissed back as best he could feeling a bit of a beginner as her hands slipped under his shirt and danced up along his backbone soft as feathers. When they broke, they were breathless and heaving and unaware that the music had stopped. Everyone around the bonfire went 'aaaah' and gave them a big round of applause, followed by whistles and cheers. He lifted Romy's hand, faced the crowd and took a bow. Romy giggled like Minnie Mouse.

'Oh, Frankie, don't be such an eejit,' she said, and he woke up.

They were walking up the old road to the Summit discussing plans for the big barbecue when Nelson suddenly wondered aloud whether or not a magnet would attract objects in space; he had been looking up at the sky last night, he said, and the thought had suddenly struck him. Frankie said that a magnet would work anywhere but Hopper told him that was rubbish.

'Of course a magnet will work in space,' Frankie said fiercely, 'it's the law of centrifugal force. Imagine not knowing that.'

'Centrifugal bolix,' Hopper sneered. 'How can a magnet attract anything in space if there's no fucken atmosphere?'

Things got heated. Nelson tried to intervene but the other two were adamant that their point of view was correct.

'I'm telling you it would,' Frankie said.

'Shite,' Hopper said.

Hopper said 'shite' to every argument that Frankie put forward. In the end, Frankie called Hopper a stupid fucking gronk and walked off with his head down.

'Hang on, will ye?' Nelson called as he and Hopper struggled to catch up, but Frankie strode on.

'All I said was that there was no gravity in space,' Hopper called. 'No need to get upset about it.'

'You said I was talking shite,' Frankie said.

'No, I didn't,' Hopper said, then hesitated while he pushed his thick round glasses back up his nose. 'OK, OK, so I did, but only because you *were* talking shite. I didn't mean it personally.'

Ahead, grey smoke drifted across the entrance to the old road to the Summit. There was a big gorse fire somewhere on the far side of the hill, but Frankie didn't care. As far as he was concerned, things were so rotten now that he didn't mind if the entire hill and everyone on it burned down. At the junction of the old road and the new, Frankie stalled.

'Don't go up the old road,' Nelson called, 'it's too dangerous.'

That made up his mind for him. Frankie plunged into the grey smoke and pounded along the old road. Nelson and Hopper yelled at him to come back out of that, but he ignored them. He was sick of being told what to do by everyone. This way at least he'd get to the Summit without having to listen to any more crap about magnets not working in space.

'Don't be so fucken stuck up,' he heard someone call dimly, from far away.

It only made him walk faster.

Within a minute, Frankie could not see two feet in front of him. The smoke stung his eyes and made him cough. He pulled his jumper up over his nose and mouth but it gave him scant protection. He kept walking, though, determined not to give in. In a little while, he was convinced the smoke would clear and he would find himself in bright sunshine just below the Summit pub. Last year he had walked through smoke from a gorse fire without a bother. And the year before as well. There were always gorse fires on the hill in summer. It was simply a matter of keeping going.

But the smoke got thicker and he began to feel weak. His legs went numb and he felt his stomach churn. Every time he coughed, more strength left him. He smacked into a wall and bounced back out into the road. This is it, he suddenly realised, I'm going to suffocate on the old road just because Hopper didn't know the first thing about centrifugal force. As he sank to his knees, he heard a strange high-pitched ring-ing in his ears. It sounded like celestial bells. Maybe he should have gone to Mass more often, he thought to himself. He prayed to God for forgiveness.

He was about to black out when a weird red-glowing spaceship appeared through the folds of grey smoke. Dark creatures with yellow heads swooped down to gather him up. He felt himself being carried through the air and plonked onto something solid which then moved off at great speed. So this is what dying is like, he thought. It wasn't half as bad as it was made out to be. Bells kept ringing over his head so he knew he was on his way to heaven.

'Thanks God,' he said.

The fire brigade dropped Frankie at the Summit. The Chief Fireman told him he was very lucky not to have done himself real damage going into a dangerous fire zone like that.

'Now go home and stay home,' the Chief Fireman said. 'I'm sick of you young fellas acting the eejit.'

Frankie promised to watch himself from now on. As the fire brigade drove off, he waved goodbye. None of the firemen waved back.

When he turned round, Hopper and Nelson were sitting on a bench outside the pub, pointing at him and giggling like monkeys. Frankie glared at them.

'Gronks,' he said, and went home to look up centrifugal force in the dictionary.

12
NELSON

Frankie woke up with the worst toothache of his life. The entire left side of his face felt as though it had been invaded by little men with flamethrowers. In the mirror, his face looked all right but he knew it was in trouble. Sooner or later he would have to go to the dentist. First, though, he had a barbecue to organise. He phoned the others and told them to start getting their acts together. It was this weekend or bust, he said firmly.

Hopper got caught trying to sneak a pig out of his Uncle Bill's butcher's shop. 'I was just checking the weight,' he explained. Uncle Bill locked Hopper in the freezer for an hour. 'Now ye can check the lot,' he said before slamming the freezer door.

Hopper came out with icy fingers and a blue nose. The first thing he did was to phone Frankie to tell him to stick his fucking barbecue. 'I'd rather stay home and watch TV—at least it doesn't give you frostbite,' he yelled.

'OK, do that then. We don't need you or your uncle's old pig anyway,' Frankie told him angrily and slammed down the phone.

At lunchtime, Davy Dudley took Frankie for a speed-run along the back roads to test out his pop's new Jaguar. He wanted to show off his brilliant reflexes.

'People keep telling me I'd make a great Grand Prix driver,' he said. 'Chicks will go mental for us when we pull up in this thing...nick-nick...'

'Don't fucken say it,' Frankie said. 'I can't stand it when you say that nicky-hooky thing.'

Davy laughed and put his foot on the accelerator. At the next corner, the great Grand Prix driver smacked his pop's brand new Jaguar into the front of a parked van. A white-haired granddad with a pipe in his mouth and five small children climbed out of the van. They surveyed the hissing wreckage.

'That was a bloody stupid thing to do, wasn't it?' the granddad said.

Davy had no tax, no insurance and no driving licence. He didn't have permission from his pop to borrow the car either. But he still smiled his broadest smile.

'I'm sure we can fix this up with me pop,' he beamed. They found Davy's pop in his back garden practising golf swings. He listened to their story with a stony face, then wrote the owner of the van a cheque and showed him to the door. After that, he went for Davy and Frankie with his golf club. 'Get the hell out of my house,' he yelled as Frankie scrambled over the back wall. 'If I ever catch you hanging around with my boy again, I'll have your kidneys for breakfast.'

In the afternoon, to cheer himself up, Frankie joined in the kickabout on the green. Nelson was in goal and Vinnie Cassidy and Nelson's brother Darwin were firing in shots at him. On the benches outside the pub, Romy Casey and Jayne

Wayne sat drinking glasses of Guinness. Jayne Wayne waved to Frankie. Romy just watched.

'What happened to the pig then?' Vinnie Cassidy jeered. 'Got cold trotters, did it?'

'Don't worry,' Frankie said casually. 'There'll be a pig at the barbecue—even if it's only you.'

'Haw fucking haw,' Vinnie shouted and kicked the ball at Frankie's face.

Frankie ducked and the ball sailed over his head into a field.

Heart pumping, he stared at Vinnie. This was the swine who had beaten him up on a regular basis ever since he could remember. This was the gap-toothed bastard who had insulted him every chance he got. This was the bullying gob-shite who was always strutting around as if he owned the hill. Enough was enough.

'Hey, get the ball—go on, run,' Vinnie said.

'Get it yourself, prickhead.'

'What did you call me?'

'Prickhead.'

'OK, you're dead, pal. Six o'clock in Plunkett's Lane, all right?'

'You're on.'

'I'm going to beat you good-looking.'

'Better make your will first.'

The kickabout lost its sparkle after that. Nelson didn't even bother to dive for shots. In a little while, Vinnie and Darwin drifted off to the pub.

'Yoo-hoo, don't forget our little date, dearie,' Vinnie called from the pub doorway and blew Frankie a kiss.

Frankie said nothing.

Nelson walked home with him. 'Well, you've done it now,' Nelson told him. 'He's gonna pull your arms and legs off.'

'I can beat him,' Frankie said, trying hard to appear cocky but feeling doomed inside; he knew if Vinnie didn't get him, the toothache would.

'I think maybe you could use a few tips,' Nelson said.

For the rest of the afternoon, Nelson had Frankie up the back garden rehearsing fighting techniques.

'Never take a wild swing,' he said. 'If you do, he'll just step inside and do this.'

Nelson stepped inside and did that and Frankie ended up on the ground.

'Will you take it easy, for fuck's sake. I'm fighting him, not you.'

'It's gotta be done,' Nelson said. 'Otherwise you're gonna get mutilated.'

By the end of the afternoon, Frankie had been dumped on the ground and slapped in the face so often his tooth didn't bother him any more; everything else in his body hurt instead.

'Think I can beat him now?'

'No, but you might irritate him a little bit.'

'Thanks. That makes me feel great.'

'Don't blame me—you got yourself into it.'

Gaptooth and the rest of the Bad Men were waiting for them at Deadman's Gulch. Gaptooth was showing off by doing high kicks.

'There goes his head,' he said as he kicked the air.

'Look out, here comes his left ball.'

None other than sheriff Bart Wyatt himself, toughest two-fisted lawman on the hill, strode down the lane cool and straight as a hero should. At his side marched deputy Paul Hindman, who was wearing his usual expression of fierce concentration. Gaptooth had been striking terror into the hearts of decent folk for too long. Now Wyatt was going to take him in. This was the final showdown.

One of the Bad Men came forward with his hands out like a preacher.

'Right, start whenever you're ready. No grabbing by the bolix and the first person to give up, loses.'

Gaptooth smiled an evil gap-toothed smile and walked forward slowly. 'Come on, son, let's go. Why didn't you bring the pig? Eh? Oink, oink, oink...'

Sheriff Bart Wyatt was no stranger to insults. The West was full of Bad Men who talked big and acted small. Bart Wyatt just smiled his prairie smile. The Bad Men guffawed. Gaptooth turned to laugh with them. Quick as lightning, the sheriff stooped, picked up a handful of dust and threw it in Gaptooth's face. Then he leaped on the outlaw, wrestled him to the ground and started punching him. Not for nothing had sheriff Bart Wyatt learned to fight dirty during the Injun Wars of '76.

'Aaaah...not fair...oooogh...'

Gaptooth spluttered as the sheriff sat on his back and pushed his face into the gravel.

'Give up?' the sheriff roared, delirious with the scent of victory and the swift decisiveness of his actions. From underneath came a grunt that sounded like 'yeah'.

Sheriff Bart Wyatt released the battered Bad Man and jumped up with his arms up like a champion.

'I won, I won,' he chanted.

'No, no, ye fucken eejit,' a voice roared.

'Whaddya mean, of course I won—he gave up, didn't he?' the sheriff asked, astonished.

The sheriff was even more astonished when Gaptooth spun him around and punched him in the nose. 'Tarnation' was all he got out before he bit the dirt.

On the ground, the sheriff had a sense of the world slipping away from him. Pain spread like gorse-fire along his mouth, teeth, eyes, nose and forehead. He tried to pull his six-shooter but the strength suddenly left him and his head slumped back. Above him, he was dimly aware of distant whacks and thumps. There was a lot of scuffling and shouting. When he raised his head, he saw two vague figures rushing at one another, merging with a thud, then breaking apart. As his vision cleared, he saw deputy Paul Hindman grab Gaptooth by the hair, force his head down and kick him several times in the face. Deputy Paul had been in the Injun wars too. Gaptooth sank to his knees and held his hands over his face. 'No more,' he sobbed. 'I give up.'

'Serves ye right, varmint,' sheriff Bart Wyatt said, and blacked out.

Next morning the sky turned purple. Then a wind struck up. Finally rain came down like shellfire. At midday, the RTE weatherman announced that coastal regions were experiencing a freak storm and that all boats should return to port immediately and stay there over the weekend.

Frankie wasn't surprised. Nothing surprised him any more. He had got used to the run of rotten luck that had destroyed his barbecue and his life. In his mind, he kissed Romy Casey goodbye for ever.

'What's the matter with your nose?' Ma said as she passed him in the hallway.

'It's nuthin. I just walked into a door, that's all.'

'You were picking at it again—I warned you it would swell up if you did.'

He went into the bathroom and examined the damage in the mirror. His nose didn't look too bad. Just a bit red around the nostrils. Last night his face had looked as though something had exploded inside it. When he had got home, Ma had been having one of her little liedowns so he hadn't had to explain himself. Even then, he had looked a lot better than Vinnie Cassidy who had a split lip, black eye, cut nose and bruised jaw. Nelson said that Vinnie's face looked as though an elephant had stepped on it. As he thought about it, Frankie smiled.

'I wouldn't look so pleased with yourself, mister,' Ma said fiercely from the bathroom doorway. 'You look like a bloody queer. Now get up the back and bring the clothes in before the storm blows them all over the hill.'

After the wind had died down, Frankie met Nelson in the Summit pub. They were trying to figure out a way to save the barbecue when the barman came over to tell them that Elvis had just died.

'Elvis Costello?' Frankie asked.

'No, ye eejit, the real Elvis.'

Nelson didn't say anything. He just drew circles in the beer froth on the counter. Frankie started to ask questions but the barman shrugged, threw up his hands and said that he'd heard it on the radio so it must be true. Then he pulled Nelson a free pint.

That was it, Frankie thought to himself; how could anyone throw a party on the weekend of the King's death. It just wasn't on.

At six, the bar-room hushed as everyone watched the news. It showed footage of Elvis in concert in Las Vegas wearing his famous white sequinned suit. Elvis was singing

'Suspicious Minds'. When it was over, Nelson sat quietly, staring deeply into his pint. From time to time, people came up to him and said, 'Sorry for your trouble.' Nelson acknowledged them with a nod of his head. There didn't seem to be any way to avoid the sad feeling, so they decided to go home.

'He was the Greatest,' Nelson said and shuffled off up the road with his head down.

On the way home, Frankie met Jayne Wayne coming in the opposite direction. She said 'Hi' and stopped to chat.

'Elvis is dead,' he announced gravely.

'Elvis Costello?'

'No, Elvis Presley. It was on the news.'

'That's terrible. Was he shot or something?'

'Heart attack, I think. It was pretty sudden anyhow.'

'That's a shame. Well, we all have to go sometime, even superstars.'

'He was more than that. He was the greatest singer in the world.'

'Maybe so. I prefer Graham Parker myself. Anyhow, are you all set for the big barbecue? I hear there's going to be a pig.'

'Er, well...the pig might have to be cancelled.

There's been a bit of hassle...'

'Well, I don't care,' Jayne said chirpily. 'If it's on, I'm going. See you then.' She flounced off towards the Summit, dark curls bouncing.

'It's real boring around here so make sure you come up with something, OK?' she called back before disappearing into the pub.

Frankie stared after her for a while, then turned and walked home. Hopper wasn't speaking to him, Davy was off-limits for life, the barbecue was a wash-out, his tooth was

killing him again, he was at war with Vinnie Cassidy, an envelope containing his exam results was due any day, California
might as well be on Jupiter and now Elvis had gone and died
...but for some reason he felt kind of good. Life was weird.
Maybe things would work out yet.

The wake was Frankie's idea.

'The King is dead, but his music will live for ever,' he said
when he phoned Nelson. 'We can meet in the Summit, then
have an Elvis night afterwards in my garage.'

After some deliberation, Nelson agreed. 'Just make sure
the electrical connections are fixed—I miss Elvis but I don't
feel like joining him just yet.'

After closing time, Nelson and Frankie and Patty Gargan
and a select few gathered in the garage for the special night
of Elvis music. Cyril McLean came too—Nelson had invited
him in a fit of sentimentality brought about by four pints of
Guinness, two whiskey-and-reds and a large Pernod. Hopper
had also been invited, but refused to have anything further
to do with Frankie's schemes, and Frankie's garage in particular. At midnight, Jayne Wayne and Jennie Brady turned up
with a bottle of wine and a six-pack of Guinness each. Jayne
gave Frankie a big wink. Stony Rogers and his flock also
showed up, but Frankie stopped them at the door.

'Sorry, no hippies.'

'That's OK, man,' said Stony, stroking his straggly locks.
'I get the vibe, but I just want you to know that I won't hold
this against you—there will always be space for you in my
house, y'know.'

They sat on rickety chairs or plonked down on discarded
car-seats, packing cases, boxes and the broken-down sofa. It
took a while to get Frankie's portable record player to

work—the speaker section was still in two jagged halves from Davy's attempts to turn it into perfect stereo. Nelson took charge of the music while Frankie set up Da's Bell and Howell 8mm silent movie projector. Cyril McLean produced a long thin joint and lit it. Everyone agreed that this was much better than trying to roast a frozen pig on a wet and windy beach.

Nelson raised a bottle of Guinness. 'To Elvis Aaron Presley, the greatest singer who ever lived. Born eighth of January, 1935, in Tupelo, Mississippi. Died today, sixteenth of August, 1977, in Graceland, Memphis, Tennessee. The King is dead. Long live the King. Amen.' Everyone solemnly toasted the King.

Nelson went to the record player and put on 'Heartbreak Hotel.' Patty Gargan jumped up on him, wrapped her legs around his waist and Nelson spun her around like a rag doll.

They listened to Elvis's Golden Records Vol 2 while they watched Charlie Chaplin clowning it up with the heavies in 'Easy Street'. Elvis's 'Sun Sessions' played while the Keystone Kops crashed and fell and skidded around corners and threw custard pies at one another. By the time Frankie showed Buster Keaton in 'The General', even Nelson was laughing and having a good time. Ma came out with a plate of hot sausages. She stayed to jive with Nelson to 'Return to Sender'. Everyone applauded and cheered when they finished. Ma never noticed the nine-skin joint Frankie was smoking or that Cyril McLean was out cold on top of a packing case.

At 2 a.m., with the wind howling outside, Buster Keaton going tickatickaticka on the wall and Elvis crooning 'This time the Girl is Gonna Stay', Frankie got off with Jayne

Wayne on the broken-down sofa. He hadn't really tried to move in on her; they had found themselves together on the sofa following a couple of wild dances and Frankie had cracked a few jokes about her flatfooted style and made her laugh and Jayne had tried to get her own back by tickling him under the arms and all of a sudden he was holding her. Just like that. The kissing sort of happened by itself. They kissed playfully at first, then tenderly. A warm hand explored his thigh. She didn't object when he slipped his hand under her blouse and worked his way up inside her bra to touch the nipple of her small firm breast.

Frankie forgot all about Romy Casey.

Daybreak came. He walked her home. At her gate, Jayne did a pirouette for him. The warm breeze whipped up her red flowing summer dress and exposed her tanned muscular legs.

'I used to be a really good ballerina—you'd know, wouldn't you?'

'Yes, of course you would,' he said.

Before they kissed goodnight, Jayne challenged him to a game of pool at the Summit next day.

'You haven't a hope,' he said, 'I'll massacre you.'

'Not if I massacre you first,' she said.

The dentist had thick black hair down both cheeks and brows that joined in the middle. He looked like a werewolf. Frankie lay back in the chair and thought about making a run for it. He didn't know which was scarier: his tooth or the dentist.

'Just open wide and relax. Sure, I wouldn't hurt a fly,' the Werewolf said and lunged at him.

Frankie had an abscess. The tooth would have to come out, but not until the swelling in the gum had gone down.

Frankie was ordered to gargle a glass of hot water and salt after every meal and before going to bed.

'Come back in a couple of days, then we'll make the bad old pain go away for ever.'

The Werewolf sent its regards to Frankie's mother.

13
JAYNE

At breakfast, Noelie threw a plate at Dawn. Then he clouted her with his can of beans. Afterwards he followed her up the back garden and bashed her on the head with a saucepan. Finally, Dawn ran teary-eyed into the kitchen. 'Mammy, Mammy, Noelie's trying to kill me.'

'Stop being silly. He's only playing. Go back out and ignore him,' Ma said and put on her coat to go to the local Fianna Fáil meeting.

Before she left, Ma told Frankie to keep an eye on things. He went into the living-room and sat in front of the large window which overlooked the small yard and back garden. Dawn was burying her dolly in the sand pit. Noelie had taken off all his clothes and was walking the back wall, chanting his 'fuck off' song. Everything seemed normal.

He thought about Jayne, the taste of her tongue and the softness of her lips. Every time he thought about her long tanned legs he got excited. He decided he was going to ask her to come to California with him when the summer was over. He could see her now, tanned and lovely in a black bikini, striding across golden sands towards him and carrying a surfboard and an ice-cream. He would become a famous rock singer or writer and she would have her own ballet company...

In a while, Noelie got down from the wall. He sneaked to within a few yards of where Dawn was playing, then flung a stone that missed her head by inches to thunk into the wall. Frankie dashed out, grabbed Noelie and smacked him hard on the bottom and across the face until he bawled.

'Don't ever hit your sister again, don't ever hit your sister again...' Frankie chanted over and over, like a drill sergeant instructing a raw recruit.

'See. Told you he was trying to bump me off,' Dawn said and carried on digging in the sand.

A little later, Noelie came over to say sorry. He even smacked himself a firm slap on the behind to show he was really serious. Frankie gave him a big hug and made him promise to be a 'good fella' from now on.

That night, Jayne met him in the back room of the Harbour Inn. They shot a few games of pool. Then they went for a walk in the park by the old castle. They found a quiet secluded spot under a bush and lay down to kiss and cuddle. He put his hand under her blouse and felt her breasts and nipples but when he tried to explore under her knickers she slapped his hand away gently.

'Ah-ah,' she scolded, 'naught-naught-naughty boy.'

Frankie wasn't sure what to say to that.

When it got dark, they went back to the bar and drank pints of Guinness and played more pool. At closing time, he walked her to her door and kissed her goodnight, but she wouldn't let go his hand. 'Come on,' she said, 'my room's at the back. Nobody will hear us.'

Giggling, she led him by the hand through the pitch-black hall, up creaking stairs and along a murky corridor to her bedroom. They stripped in the dark, climbed into her squeaky bed and fumbled and groped and grappled with each other in the moonlight that was shining into the room. Frankie made mad dashes to the window whenever he thought he heard footsteps outside the door. Throughout, his penis remained as soft as a spent balloon. Jayne petted, pulled, massaged, tugged, caressed and finally put her mouth on it, but it refused to get hard. It was ironic, Frankie thought—all the nights of fantasising about naked girls and when he finally had a shot at the real thing his tool went on strike.

Typical.

'Don't worry, it happens all the time,' Jayne said, but that only made him feel worse.

That afternoon, Maggie stomped into the kitchen, hauling Pierre in after her by the arm. Pierre had his hands covering his face so only a pair of squinting eyes were visible.

'Look what your friend Nelson Fitzgerald did just now at the Summit,' Maggie said fiercely.

'What?' Frankie sneered.

'He hit Pierre just because he said that John Lennon was better than Elvis. I think he broke his nose. Some friends you've got.'

Frankie was stunned. Pierre was a complete gronk, but he was still his sister's boyfriend. If anyone had a right to hit him it was Frankie. Clobbering Vinnie Cassidy had clearly gone to Nelson's head.

'Look at this,' Maggie said and tilted Pierre's head back to expose his bloody nostrils. 'That Nelson's a savage.'

'S'alright' Pierre said weakly. 'Lease Dye can dill breed.'

At the Summit, Nelson was lounging against the wall with his brother Darwin and Cyril McLean giving hard looks to everyone who walked by.

'Howarya,' he said when Frankie approached. 'I was just going to call for you.'

Frankie ignored him and walked by to the shops.

'What's the matter with you?' Nelson called.

When Frankie came out of the shops carrying a bottle of milk and ten Major, Nelson was waiting with a big smile.

'Listen, what's up?'

'You can't go around hitting people.'

'He said Lennon was better than Elvis, for fuck's sake.'

'It's still stupid.'

'I know. He was a fucken eejit to say it.'

'That's not what I meant.'

'So what are you going to do about it?'

Frankie kept walking. 'Let's just pretend we never met, OK?'

'Aw, for fuck's sake...'

'You've caused enough trouble. Leave me alone.'

'All right, be like that then. You Griffins are so bloody stuck up.'

Frankie walked on, feeling hard and cold and determined and a bit sick. Nelson had gone too far. It was about time someone stood up to him. He was only doing it for Nelson's own good.

Halfway down the road, Frankie heard a shout. 'Hey, I made a big mistake. I should have hit *you*.'

* * *

On Sunday morning, Frankie spent an hour in the bathroom, washing his hair and squeezing the blackheads on his face in order to make a good impression on Jayne's parents. He had on his best blue jeans, new white shirt, black slimjim tie and the pale cream coloured evening jacket he'd bought in Capel Street for a fiver. He was convinced it made him look like James Bond. On his feet were a pair of tattered runners, but he was sure Jayne's mother wouldn't bother looking down. When Ma saw his get up, she was positive he was in trouble with the Law.

'No, I'm not going to court,'he explained. 'I've been invited to dinner at Jayne's.'

'Oh, imagine that! Your own family isn't good enough for you on Sundays any more, is that it?'

'Oh God,' Frankie said, and ran to catch the hill bus.

Jayne lived in a pink two-storied square-roofed house by the sea. There were three shiny black Mercedes and a jeep in the driveway. The front doorbell chimed like a grandfather clock. For a moment, Frankie felt like going home and forgetting the whole business. Just then the door opened. Jayne was delighted to see Frankie.

'Mum, Mum,' she called out, 'guess who's here?'

Jayne's mother turned out to be a smaller version of Jayne. She had the same big brown eyes, the same sharp nose and the same dizzy smile. She shook his hand enthusiastically and gave him a peck on the cheek.

'Call me "Mum",' she chirped. 'After all, we're really quite family now, aren't we?'

A tall old man with a scrinched-up face stooped into the hallway and peered at Frankie through thick black glasses that made his eyes look like searchlights. He was dressed in a shaggy woollen jumper and loose tweed trousers that ballooned at the knees. A black briar pipe that looked as though it had been chewed by a dog bobbed up and down in his tight mouth.

'Samuel, say hello to Francis,' Mum said.

Samuel grunted. 'If you really care for my daughter, you'll marry her and that's that,' he whined, in the thinnest, highest voice Frankie had ever heard.

'Oh, Samuel. That's not very nice now, is it?' Mum tittered and smiled nervously at Frankie to show him that everything was grand really.

'Don't care. Had my say,' Samuel squeaked as he shuffled off into the dining-room.

'Don't mind him,' Jayne whispered. 'He's always like this at first. You'll soon get to know one another and then you'll be chums.'

'Chums?' Frankie said.

The dining room was a long rambling rectangular affair with a slippery wooden floor that echoed footsteps like cannonfire. There were alcoves and crannies housing hanging plants, small potted trees, stumpy cacti, vases of dried flowers and various shrubs and greenery. Jayne's family sat around the table, staring at one another like embalmers waiting for the next body to be wheeled in.

Jayne introduced Frankie to her older sisters: pudgy, curly-headed Marjorie and dumpy, red-faced Phyllis. Both twittered 'hello'. Next came Marjorie's droopy-looking husband Ronald, and Phyllis's small, fidgety husband, Hans.

'Hans is from Hanover,' Mum explained and Hans beamed.

'Ja, Hanover,' he agreed.

'Isn't Francis scrummy?' Jayne asked and her sisters said 'yes,' 'isn't he just,' 'rather,' 'very scrummy indeed'.

Older brother Lennie was Afro-haired with a shaggy red beard and a nose like a pickaxe. Lennie's skinny girlfriend Gerty had a long-drawn face and a nervy flickering smile.

'Y'alright?' Lennie said, as he jerked the ringtag from a can of Heineken, spraying Gerty with froth.

Frankie and Jayne took their seats. Suddenly, Mum raced from the room. She returned moments later carrying a silver platter with a large steaming turkey on it.

'Oooh,' everyone said.

Lennie finished his can, crumpled it, and belched.

'Oh, Leonard,' Mum said.

'S'alright,' Lennie growled.

Samuel stood up from the table and held his hands together on the silver carving knife which pointed downward at the bloated turkey. Everyone looked at the tablecloth. Samuel cleared his throat and began to say grace in his whiney voice.

'Lord, please accept our thanks for this food which is on this table which we are about to eat. We would also like to take this opportunity to thank our wonderful Mum who prepared this fine feast. We would also like to give thanks we are all alive on this sabbath day in order that we may celebrate your holiness. We also give thanks for your kindness in giving Jayne the inspiration to prepare the delicious stuffing...'

Samuel whined on and on. Frankie felt a bubble of laughter rising in his throat. He tried to think of something serious as a distraction, but suddenly Samuel was thanking the Lord for the potatoes and the greens and the wine and Frankie had to fight hard to control himself.

He thought about games of football on the green and walking the cliff paths at night, and about Noelie clocking people on the head with his can of beans...

He was doing fine, until Samuel praised the Lord for the 'glorious gravy'. The sound that suddenly burst out of Frankie's mouth was a cross between a snort and a very loud hiccup. It made everyone jump and caused Gerty to spill her wine.

'Gosh, sorry,' Gerty said. 'I'm such an oaf.'

'Never mind,' Mum said, dashing from her chair. 'I'll get a cloth and have it cleaned up in a jiffy.'

'Excuse me,' Frankie said and gave a polite cough.

'...A-men,' Samuel said, glaring down at him. Then he raised the knife and leaned over to carve the turkey.

Frankie was handed a plate with a thin slice of turkey breast on it, flanked by two small roast potatoes, a scatter of peas and a spoonful of stuffing. There was a tiny splash of brown gravy behind one of the potatoes. As they were handed their plates, the others went 'ooh' and 'aah' and 'oh, golly'. Everyone waited with forks upraised. Samuel nodded and eating commenced.

Frankie made three incisions, raised his fork to his mouth half a dozen times and his plate was bare.

'Is that it or what?' he whispered to Jayne. 'How about seconds?'

Jayne told him to wait until everyone else was finished. The others took a long time to clear their plates. It seemed to Frankie that the slower they ate, the more content they were. Food was sometimes speared on forks and poised in mid-air, only to be put back down again. Jayne's sisters chattered to Mum about kids and cats and woolly jumpers with designs on them. Ronald and Hans lowered glass after glass of wine and talked to Samuel about cars. Lennie drank cans of Heineken from his personal collection of six-packs under the table. He didn't offer a can to Frankie.

When everyone had finished, Samuel nodded to Mum who rose from the table and carried off the remains of the turkey. As she passed Frankie, she smiled.

'This will do grand for tomorrow's stew,' she whispered conspiratorially. 'Might even get the week out of it.'

Frankie watched the turkey being whisked out of the door and felt his stomach boom. Beside him, Gerty accidentally dropped her cigarette into her glass of wine, then panicked and yanked the glass off the table into her lap.

'Oh, I'm just such a clod, really I am.'

Mum, just back from stashing the turkey, said not to worry and fussed out of the door to get a napkin. Frankie turned and found Lennie grinning hugely at him.

'Owzitgoin', y'alright?' Lennie barked.

'M'alright,' Frankie barked back.

Dessert was a small portion of ice cream in a bowl the size of an egg cup. It didn't take long. Frankie finished his in one go. After that, Mum dragged everyone off to the lounge for coffee and singing.

'Singing?' Frankie whispered.

'You'll love it,' Jayne said. 'Wait and see.'

In the lounge, they sat around on wooden benches while Gerty tinkled the piano and Samuel began to sing a selection from Gilbert and Sullivan. Frankie wanted to leave the moment Gerty hit the first resounding plonk; her playing sounded like suet pudding being hurled into a wall. Samuel sang as though something were dying in his throat. At the end of an hour, Frankie had gone off music for good.

Afterwards, Jayne walked him to the bus stop.

'So,' she said cheekily, 'now that you've met my family, when do I get to meet yours?'

'We'll see,' he said.

14

MA

On Friday night, Frankie brought Jayne home. They all watched the late horror films on TV. Ma brought in a pot of tea and bacon sandwiches. Ray turned down the volume and put smart remarks into the mouths of the characters. Everyone laughed. Jayne thought Ray was 'quite cute'. Frankie was delighted it was going so well.

Midway through '*The Bride of Dracula*', Ma moved her chair next to Jayne's.

'Where's your mother from?'

'Belfast.'

'A wonderful city. It'll soon be free again, thank God.'

Frankie felt his stomach tighten.

'And your father?'

'He's from Essex. But he's been living here for twenty years now.'

Even Dracula froze solid.

Ma stood up, snatched up all the cups and put them back on the tray, even though Jayne hadn't finished drinking her tea. Then she swept from the room. A few seconds later, the kitchen door slammed so hard the house shook.

'Was it something I said?' Jayne asked.

'It's late. Maybe we should go,' Frankie said.

Frankie walked Jayne home. Then he took a stroll up to the head and back. After that he sat on the low wall outside the Summit pub and smoked a cigarette. On the way home, he dawdled at gates, fences, and by the entrances to fields. At the top of his road he spent ten minutes chasing a cat.

It didn't make any difference.

When he got back all the front lights were blazing and Ma was waiting for him in the study. The second he was in the door she lit on him, demanding to know why he had brought a Brit into *her* home. Did he not realise that Ireland had suffered under the yoke of the Sassenachs for over eight hundred years? How could he do something like this to his own mother? Was he cracked or what?

'But Ma, Jayne is Irish,' he protested.

'Ha, indeed she's not. How could she be Irish with a name like Jayne? Would you cop yourself on, mister. Her father is a Brit—she said so herself. Therefore she's a Brit too. Her mother is obviously a proddie planter from Belfast – who else would marry a Brit from Essex? When I think of all the noble Irishmen who gave their lives up north for Mother Ireland and then my own son brings home a Brit bitch.'

'Don't call her a bitch, she's not a bitch.'

'*Bitch, Bitch, Bitch...*'

Frankie walked out of the room into the kitchen, but Ma followed him, chanting 'bitch' as loudly as she could. Her eyes were red and her face was contorted. He was afraid to look at her. He tried to go back into the hall but she stood in front of the door and blocked him.

'Oooh, yes, try and dodge,' she said in triumph, 'Don't scrinch your face up at me, if you please. No Brit bitch is going to come between an Irish Celtic warrior mother and her eldest son.'

'She's not a British bitch, she's an Irish bitch.'

'*How dare you contradict your own mother.* Who would have thought that my own flesh and blood would have turned out to be a dirty Brit-lover. You're as bad as the dirty Black and Tans. What about the 1916 Rising when Jayne's father's countrymen shot dead thousands of innocent Irish revolutionaries? What about Father Murphy's glorious Rising of 1798? What about Wolfe Tone and poor old Robert Emmet? Look what they did to Parnell.'

'Wolfe Tone was a proddie.'

'Oh my God,' Ma gasped and put her hand to her mouth. 'I suppose she told you that, did she?'

'No. He just was. And so was Casement and Parnell and Emmet. They couldn't help it. Didn't stop them being Irish.'

'I don't believe God could be so cruel to me. I can't believe I'm hearing English Government propaganda in my own house, from my own son. I should have used the wooden spoon to you more when you were younger. I suppose Pearse was a Brit too. And De Valera. Have you forgotten the fact that it was the Brits who starved millions of our people to death during the Great Famine just so's they could use our crops to make cakes for the fat bitch of an English queen across the water?'

'There was no famine. That was just a Hollywood myth,' Frankie heard himself saying.

Ma's jaw dropped, just as Frankie knew it would. She stood staring at him in bug-eyed horror for a few silent moments. Then her eyes narrowed and she nodded as though everything had suddenly become very clear.

'Your mind's gone. She's taken possession of you. I should have thrown her out of here the second I laid eyes on her. There was something queer-looking in that tight devious little face of hers—the wagon. I should have poured the Lourdes water Auntie Betty sent me all over that conniving curly head.'

Ma flopped against the mantelpiece in anguish. Within seconds she was sobbing loudly. She held her head back so the tears could flow without hindrance. Then she put her hand up to her forehead and closed her eyes.

'I've not long to go because of all the worry—I can feel my life slipping away.'

As soon as Ma began wailing again, Frankie escaped into the hallway. Ma followed him. He dashed down the corridor into his own room, but Ma charged the door as he was trying to close it and forced her way in, flicking on the light and calling Frankie a traitor and roaring out about the Brits and the Black and Tans and the proddie landowner planters and the Irish civil service who were no more than Brits in disguise and the Fine Gael fascist blueshirt bastard Figgises next door who were out to turn the Celts back into peasants.

Ray jumped up in his bed. Like everyone else in the house, Ray had been awake all along listening to the row, but now he pretended to have been out cold. 'What's going on?' he said.

Ma told him to shut his face and go back to sleep. 'I'm explaining things to your older brother.'

Frankie skipped out the door, evaded Ma's lunge, and ran back down the corridor into the study. Before he could close the door, Ma was in behind him. She barked in triumph. 'Now! How dare you leave a room before I'm finished talking to you. Look at you with all that filthy hair hanging down your neck. I've a good mind to have you fumigated.'

'I'm leaving and I'm never coming back.'

'Oh, are you now?' Ma threw back her head and laughed a loud raucous forced laugh. 'Try it,' she said. 'Just try it, mister.'

Then she started going on about his clothes, his habits, his diction, his bathroom etiquette, his acne, his dirty fingernails, his disgusting taste in music, his future, his dandruff and the dirty socks she kept finding under his bed which were stained with God knows what. Next she reached into her apron pocket and triumphantly pulled out a crumpled three-pack of Durex contraceptives. One gold-foil-wrapped circle peeped out of the squashed pack. 'I found these filthy things in the pocket of your other jacket. Do you go around abusing the holy tabernacle of a woman's body with contraceptives, do you? *Do you? Did you commit sex with a Brit? Did you? Hah?* Answer me now.'

He kept looking around for an escape route but Ma stood in front of the door and he knew he'd never get a window open in time. He felt like a six-year-old waiting to be whacked.

Ma threw the Durex into the fireplace. 'They'll stay there until your father gets home—then we'll see.'

She started on about the Brits and the glorious IRA and how mixed marriages between proddies and paddies never worked. He let it all pass. Even the stuff about Jayne having taken possession of his mind didn't bother him any more.

But when she said she was bringing him before the priest first thing in the morning to get him exorcised, he told her she was crazy.

'Oh I am, am I? I'll tell you something, mister highfalutin Francis Griffin. You come directly from the High Kings of Tara and your bloodline is one of the most revered in Europe. Professors of history and archaeology and scientists from all over the world would give their eye teeth to have just a bottle of our blood to study but I wouldn't part with it, no way. We're a respectable family.'

'What are you going on about?'

'I'm talking about history, you stupid boy. Aah, you wouldn't understand.'

Suddenly, Ma began to sob again. 'When I think of all the love I put into you and all the hours slaving away on your behalf, cooking your dinners and breakfasts and teas without a word of complaint, dressing you and darning your socks and buying you underwear and wiping your little bottom for you...and this is the thanks I get—stabbed in the heart by my own firstborn son...'

'Why are you making such a fuss? She's just my girlfriend.'

Ma gave him a look. *No, she is not. She's the bitch who's taken my son!* she yelled. Ma picked up the bronze bust of Cuchulain from the mantelpiece and flung it. He ducked and it crashed into the door.

'For God's sake...'

Ma made a grab at him but he slapped her hands away. She looked at her hands in wide-eyed disbelief. Then her eyes flickered...'You've laid hands on your own mother. The Bible says that any son who raises a hand to his own mother will burn in hellfire for eternity. Right, I'm getting the wooden spoon.'

Ma pushed past him and stalked out of the room and down the hall. Frankie heard her rummaging in the kitchen drawer. He decided to get out while he could. Maybe she wouldn't be able to find the wooden spoon and would come back at him with a kitchen knife or something. He ran from the room and yanked open the front door, just as Ma rushed into the hallway and went for him. He could feel something swish past as he ran down the steps in the dark and leaped the hedge into the garden. He didn't stop until he reached the white posts at the bottom of the drive.

When he looked back, he saw Ma in the light from the open doorway, darting in and out of the house, hurling objects out into the darkness after him. A book clunked onto the tarmac. Then a picture frame smashed on the path. His brand new Stranglers album went gliding over his head into Figgis's garden. Within moments, every album he owned seemed to be flying through the air. He recognised the sleeve of 'The Allman Brothers Live at the Fillmore East' just before it thudded into the telegraph pole above his head and went spiralling off into the blackness

'You're no son of mine. I hereby banish you from this house for ever. Don't come back. Go and stay with your British slut — if she'll have you. It wouldn't surprise me if the *bitch* let you get her pregnant just so's she could have a Griffin child to blackmail us with.'

She took off her slippers and flung them too. When she had nothing more to throw she turned awkwardly on her stockinged heels, tossed back her hair and walked smack into the wall. She wobbled once, then went in.

The front door slammed like a gunshot.

Frankie tried to sleep on the broken-down sofa in the garage, but no matter which way he turned, there was always something sticking into him. Much later he heard soft voices coming from the kitchen. He was sure they were talking about him, so he got up, crossed the yard on tiptoe and peeped in through the kitchen window. Ma and Maggie were sitting at the kitchen table. Ma had her head down. She sobbed softly with her long hair flowing out across the table while Maggie stroked her hands and told her that it was OK.

Ma looked up with wet red eyes and a tear-streaked face. It was just that tonight was Clara's birthday, she said; she always remembered and every year it got worse. Clara had been such a beautiful little thing, and she had only lived an hour then she was gone and nobody could tell her why—not even the doctors, not Da, not Granny, not anyone...Tonight, Clara would have been nineteen years old. It was all this remembering that had her in a bad mood...and then there was poor Noelie...it just wasn't fair...she had a lot of crosses to bear for her family, it was just too much sometimes...'I know, I know,' Maggie said, 'it's OK now, I'll make a cup of tea.' Ma put her head down again. 'She was such a beautiful little thing,' Ma said.

Frankie went back to the garage feeling sad and weak and guilty. Later, as he thought things over, he grew angry again. He couldn't put off a decision any longer, he knew; tomorrow he would go to the bank and draw out all his bulb-picking money and buy a plane ticket for California—a one-way ticket. He wouldn't even say goodbye. He wouldn't leave a note, either. That would shake them. Instead, he would send Ma a postcard from America. Things had just gone too far now; there was nothing for him at home any more.

Towards dawn, when the lights were off in the kitchen and there was no sound in the house, he tapped on his bedroom window until Ray woke up and let him in. He lay on his bed with all his clothes on, afraid to go to sleep in case he dreamed about Clara in the attic. Hours later, he finally dropped off into fitful, uneasy sleep. He had no dreams at all.

When Frankie got up, there was a priest waiting for him in the front room.

'This is Father Murphy, a dear friend of the family,' Ma said and left them.

Father Murphy was small and squat and wore a lopsided blond hairpiece. He looked like a gargoyle from the church roof. Frankie had never laid eyes on him before.

Father Murphy grinned at Frankie. 'Ah yes, Frankie. I hear you haven't been feeling yourself lately.'

'Huh?' Frankie said.

Ma reappeared carrying a bowl of water. She smiled a knowing smile.

Father Gargoyle advanced on Frankie holding a large crucifix. 'Now, this isn't going to hurt a bit, just blank your mind and think of God.'

Frankie wasn't sure what was going on, but he knew he didn't want to be a part of it. Ma was standing with her back to the door, face stern and lips set in a triumphant grin. A clammy hand descended on his scalp, gripping it firmly and pushing his head down. He knew it wasn't a dream because he could feel his hair being pulled out by the roots. Father Gargoyle forced Frankie into a kneeling position and started chanting.

'Out, demon, out, in the name of the Lord. Get thee behind me, Satan.'

'Aaaagh, leave me alone, will ye?'

'Ha, that's not my son speaking, Father. I knew he was possessed the second I saw him with that Brit bitch.'

Frankie tried to break free but Father Gargoyle held on tight. In the struggle, the bowl of water was sent splooshing across the floor. Frankie's head smacked into something hard. The crucifix looped through the air and hit the carpet with a thunk.

Ma shrieked. 'Christ, he's trying to desecrate the holy cross.'

Ma picked up the crucifix, then pressed it into Frankie's forehead. From the corner of a teary eye, Frankie saw Maggie and Ray appear in the doorway. Dawn's fair head peeped around Ray's shoulder but Maggie turned and pushed her out.

'Aw, I wanna see Francis doing his exercise,' Dawn cried. 'S'not fair.'

Suddenly all the fight left Frankie and he slumped in the priest's arms. This was the end, he realised; this was the punishment for all the sins he had ever committed. Every bad, twisted, depressing feeling he had ever felt in his life flooded back into him now and made him feel weak and rotten and useless. There was no doubt in his mind that he was doomed; the best he could hope for was to burn in hell for eternity. Ma and Father Gargoyle were right, he thought; he really was possessed by the Devil. This was Judgment Day for all the drinking and partying and dope-smoking and hanging around with bad company like Davy Dudley and Hopper Delaney. He was bad through and through: he never went to Mass or took a bit of notice of anything religious. He remembered all the Sunday mornings when Ma had tried to get him out of bed to go to Mass and he had ignored her, sometimes letting on to be sick in order to stay on in bed. How could he have been so wicked? Ma had been so good to him and he had treated her appallingly. It was obvious to him now that his entire life had been filled with mortal sins. Going out with a Protestant had been the final abomination. Now, look where it had got him: he was on his knees in the front room with his mother screaming at him and a priest he had never seen before in his life attempting to pull his head off. Maybe none of this would have happened, he thought sadly, if only he'd given up wanking.

Then Father Gargoyle belched into Frankie's face. A blast of rancid whiskey breath instantly brought Frankie's strength surging hack. Suddenly he was angry. Very angry. The feelings of guilt dissolved as though they had never existed. He realised that he was being humiliated in his own house for no reason and that made him mad at Ma and the priest and Mr Vincent and Mrs Donovan from down the road and the Freedom Fighter and the rest of Ma's friends—and even Da over in America.

With all his heart, he knew that he had done nothing wrong. He didn't deserve to have a crazy priest screaming Latin gibberish into his ear like a demented parrot. It was time he stood up for himself. Jayne Wayne was his girlfriend. That was the way it was and that was the way it was going to stay. Nobody—not even Ma—was going to break them up. It didn't matter that Jayne was a Protestant. Being a Protestant didn't mean a person was wicked. There were lots of Protestants in the world and they couldn't all be evil. He knew that as sure as he knew he was kneeling there. He might turn Protestant himself if he got out of this situation alive—just to get his own back. He was sure God would understand.

Right now he was going to fight for Jayne and for all of his friends and even his brothers and sisters who didn't know enough or were too scared to stand up for themselves. Most of all, though, he was going to fight for himself. No drunken priest was going to tell him that he was possessed by a demon. It was all Ma's fault. She was doing this to get him back because he wouldn't do what she wanted. Well, he wasn't going to let her get away with it any longer. He was seventeen going on eighteen and it was high time he started acting like an adult instead of a kid.

He pushed himself forward with a last great effort, taking Father Gargoyle in mid-chant.

'Ah, Jaysis,' Father Gargoyle cried as they caroomed off the fireplace and hit the bookcase.

'He's too strong for us—I knew I should have got a bishop!' Ma shouted before she went over too.

They crashed to the floor in a shower of books and papers and dust. Father Gargoyle's wig landed on the heater. In seconds, smoke began to rise from it.

Frankie wriggled to the foot of Da's big black leather arm-chair with Father Gargoyle riding on his back like a cowboy, eyes closed, muttering in prayer. Ma was wrapped around his legs and was dragged along behind, yelling for somebody to send for a guard, for God's sake. Somehow, he twisted free and made it to Da's desk where he seized a letter-knife. Holding it out in front of him, he crouched waiting for the others to attack. He yelled that he wasn't going to take it any more, that he was a good person and Jayne Wayne was a good person and all of his friends were good people and Mr Figgis from next door was a good person too. He pointed the letter-knife at Ma.

'If anyone in this room needs to be exorcised, it's you!' he shouted.

'Ha, listen to him. My son, the demon,' Ma hissed, scrambling to her feet.

Ma and Father Gargoyle slowly advanced on him. Father Gargoyle's eyes were bright as he held the sharp end of the crucifix in front of him like a sword.

The doorbell rang.

Everyone stopped and looked at each other. In a few seconds, the bell chimed again.

'I'll get it,' Ray said cheerfully, and ran out to open the door.

The door slammed and a moment later Ray was back with a long white envelope in his hands. He came forward and beamed at Frankie.

'That was the postman with a special delivery. It's your exam results,' he said, waving the envelope.

Frankie fainted.

When he came to, he was lying on his bed with all his clothes on and Ma was above him waving a piece of paper down at him. She was beaming from ear to ear and jumping about like a girl. Frankie was sure the priest had sent him to hell.

'My son, the professor of history,' Ma said and bent down to shake his hand. 'I always knew you wouldn't let your family down.'

Ray and Dawn helped Frankie up. Father Gargoyle was nowhere in sight.

'You got three honours,' Ray said. 'English, Irish and History. Pretty neat, huh?'

'Are you going to uni now?' Dawn asked, but Frankie was still too stunned to answer.

'Of course he is,' Ma snapped. 'It's the High King blood. A thoroughbred always wins through in the end. You'll end up President of Ireland. I always knew it.'

'Where's the priest?' Frankie asked.

Ma looked at him as though he'd lost his mind. 'What priest?' she said puzzled, then suddenly frowned. 'Oh, he had to go. Never mind that now.'

Then she waved the piece of paper in the air and danced a jig around the study, singing 'diddle-ee-eye-dill, diddle-ee-eye-dill...'

The others took Frankie by the hands and made him dance too.

Later, Da rang from New York to say that all his scenes had been shot and he was flying home next day. Ma told him about Frankie's exam results and Da said it was very good news and well done and that he'd bring him home an extra LP tomorrow.

'Mind you,' Ma reflected afterwards, 'you could have got an honour in Geography, too. It wouldn't have killed you, you know.'

As soon as the shock had worn off, Frankie slipped out the back door and walked around the garden. There was nobody about. Over the back wall, he could see deserted fields of yellow and brown bracken swinging in the breeze, all the way up to the rocks. For the first time in a long while, maybe for the first time ever, he felt in charge of his life. The paper with the exam results was bunched into the back pocket of his jeans. He took it out and uncrumpled it for another look. It made him proud to see his name at the top and under it the grades that meant that he hadn't made a balls of things after all.

It was funny how things worked out. All summer he had tried not to think about exams or college. It had never occurred to him that he could actually succeed at anything. Instead, he had imagined people lining up to sneer at his fail-ure—Ma, Vinnie Cassidy, the Rumpus Gran and Auntie Lucy, Maggie and Ray, various Christian Brothers, even the ghost of Buster's prettiest kitten. A little while ago, a drunken priest had been attempting to drive the Devil out of him and now here he was with three honours and Ma praising him to the skies and Da coming home from America with albums for him. You wouldn't think there had ever been any trouble at all. Even last night's big row with Ma seemed so long ago and far off that it might just as well have happened to another Frankie in another life.

In the morning, the house was shining like a new kettle. A roast was sizzling in the oven and the living-room was sparkling with the best silver and china. Ma sent everyone out in shifts to watch out for Da's taxi.

It felt like a Big Day.

Frankie sat on the porch, thinking things over. California could wait, he decided. There was no point going anywhere just now. He had a good feeling inside. For the first time in a long while, he was at peace. There were lots of things to do and he could do them just as well at home as anywhere else. Well, for the time being anyway. He felt great. It didn't even bother him when he saw Jayne Wayne shooting up the road on the back of Bobby Gallo's Kawasaki. There were other girls on the hill. Jennie Brady had been giving him looks lately, he had noticed. And there was still Romy Casey. Anything was possible now. He had stacks of time. In a while, he might even give Nelson a ring.

Dawn came out to join him. She sat down beside him, her little face grave.

'Noelie never hits me now,' she said.

'That's good.'

'Are you still going away to California?'

'I might.'

Dawn's face dropped.

'Then again, I might not.'

'Well, I think you should stay and go to uni.'

Frankie laughed. 'I might.'

Dawn smiled and her face relaxed. 'Good,' she said.

When Da's taxi roared up the driveway, everyone came rushing out to the porch. His massive frame was squeezed into the front seat, twisting around to wave to them through the side window. In the back seat, they could see piles of suit-cases and bags and boxes.

'Wave, everybody wave,' Ma said, her face shining. 'Show your father what a great family he has.'

Everyone waved.